JUST A BITE

Boris Bacic

BUTTERDRAGONS
PUBLISHING

I feel them moving
Crawling inside me

Decaying
Rotting

Devouring my organs
Weakening me

My mind is crumbling
Hope is far away

by Helle Gade

LAB PART 1

Phillip gave a curt nod to the security guard as the gate slid open. He didn't wait to see if the guard would greet him back, and instead drove onto the company grounds. Sleep still crusted Phillip's eyes. He had to rub them and blink hard to chase the nagging drowsiness awake.

Just twenty minutes earlier, he had received a call that awoke him from a pleasant dream. He couldn't tell what the dream had been about, but whatever it was, he didn't appreciate being awoken at two in the morning.

People stood in front of the building where he worked. The way they all faced him, Phillip could tell they were waiting just for him. He recognized Doctor Simmons' lab pristine lab coat in the scintillating light. The other two figures who stood around him were dressed fully in black, assuming wide-legged stances, with assault rifles in their hands.

When he first started working here, the sight of armed men made him feel uneasy. His hand trembled whenever he presented his ID card to them. He never had problems with them, and eventually, seeing the armed security forces was as normal as saying "good morning" to a co-worker in the company's kitchen.

Phillip parked his car in front. The eyes of Doctor Simmons scrupulously followed him. Phillip killed the engine and stepped outside. It was chilly, and it would only be slightly better inside the office.

Hasty footsteps approached him as he locked his car. Already, he was starting to feel like the entire company was breathing down his neck.

"Doctor Curtis. Thank you so much for coming down here on such short notice," Simmons said as he stopped right in front of Phillip.

Phillip turned to face him. It was difficult not to notice the enormous, bug-like glasses that Doctor Simmons wore, which always hung at the tip of his nose. He was a man in his forties with slick hair and a clean-shaven face that showed his flabby cheeks. For a while, he spoke about growing a beard, but due to company policy, he was unable to do so.

"Not like I had a choice," Phillip replied. "I trust you have something important to show me, yes? Otherwise, dragging me out of bed at such an ungodly hour can wait."

"I apologize for calling you at this time, Doctor Curtis. I assure you that this matter is *very* important," Simmons said, pushing the glasses up his nose with the tip of his forefinger.

"Very well. Let's see it," Phillip said.

He still had no idea what this was about. His work encompassed such a wide spectrum that guessing what might be the urgency tonight would be the same as guessing next week's lottery numbers.

Doctor Simmons spun on his heel and broke into a stride toward the building where the armed figures stood. Phillip dug through his pocket and got his ID card ready. Simmons walked between the two giants and the double doors at the entrance parted ways for him.

Phillip presented the card to one of the masked figures, who in turn, simply nodded and gestured toward the building with the barrel of his rifle. Okay, no need for such scrutiny tonight, great.

Simmons was already inside the corridor, impatiently waiting for Phillip to catch up. Phillip put the ID card in his pocket and stepped inside. The electronic doors closed behind him, muffling the outside noises.

Just as Phillip suspected, it was almost as cold inside as it was outside. The company didn't invest too much into heating, but given the nature of the work, it was understandable. Warm temperatures could cause a lot of problems at the office, even with all the other precautions in place.

"Don't worry about wearing a lab coat, Doctor," Simmons said, apprehending Phillip's thoughts. "The company won't mind it tonight. Right now, they just want you on site, ASAP."

The company had a strict rule that every employee on the science and Research and Development team had to wear a sterilized lab coat at all times. The first time an employee was caught without one, he got a warning. The next time, a suspension. Three strikes and they're out.

"So, wanna tell me what this is all about, Doctor Simmons?" Phillip asked, impatience that had been simmering inside him this entire time now reaching a boiling temperature.

One sentence summarizing everything would suffice. There was no need for such a dramatic build-up.

"I believe it's best if you see with your own eyes, Doctor Curtis," Simmons replied brusquely as he led Phillip down the hall.

They went through more electronic doors, turning left, then right, going in the direction of the lab. It always took a long time getting from one end to the other. When Phillip first started working, his lunch breaks made him feel like he needed to do sprints to make it in time to the cafeteria and back.

The company had a strict lunch break from 1 P.M. to 2 P.M. for all employees with some exceptions, and they were not permitted to leave the company premises until work was done.

Prior to that, Phillip liked having his lunch around noon, so having to readjust to a later lunch was a pain. The fact that he didn't need to pay for his own lunch anymore, coupled with the fact that the food served was top quality, he didn't complain.

When they finally reached the research section, Phillip slowed down. But Doctor Simmons walked right past it as if it wasn't even there. For the first time that night, Phillip's heart began racing.

Only one more destination remained at the end of the corridor – the quarantine section.

He hurried his pace. He wanted to stop Doctor Simmons right then, shake him by the collar, and demand to know what was going on. Instead, he strode on, now struggling to keep up the pace with Simmons. His legs felt brittle, like that time when he ran an ultramarathon.

Up until the point when they reached the doors leading into quarantine, Phillip firmly believed that this wasn't the right destination. Just as the doors parted ways, Simmons turned around and trained his eyes on Phillip.

"Ready, Doctor Curtis?" he asked.

Phillip nodded in approval. They entered. Simmons walked over to the thick pane of glass on the other side of the room and turned to look at Phillip in a "follow me" motion. Phillip approached and peered through the glass. His jaw dropped to the floor.

"My God," was all he could utter.

PRELUDE

"Why are you still here? You're going to be late," Catherine, my roommate, said.

She was sitting on the couch, bundled up in her pajamas and tucked under a thick blanket. A show was running on the TV in the background. I kind of felt jealous. I'd been looking forward to my date with Darren all week long, but now that the time had finally come, I really just wanted to stay inside and watch the show with Catherine despite having no idea what it was about, what episode she was on, or how many seasons it had.

I didn't even like watching shows.

"Melanie." Catherine raised an eyebrow at me. "Are you getting cold feet?"

"No." I bit my lip. "Maybe. Kind of."

The palm resting on my handbag was clammy and I was sure the heat of the apartment had nothing to do with it. Catherine let out an exasperated sigh and threw the blankets aside. She stood and walked up to me.

I can't imagine how difficult it must have been for her to separate from the warm sanctuary of the couch.

She put her hands on my shoulders and flashed me a reassuring smile. "It'll be fine," she said. "You and Darren already know each other. You like each other. You're just two people going out for dinner to get to know each other a little better. If the date goes great, awesome. If not..." She shrugged. "Who cares? Not like we live in a tribe where there's a limited number of men."

Easy for you to speak. You're staying home watching shows, I thought to myself. It wouldn't be fair of me to say it aloud, especially since Catherine was trying to give me a pep talk before my date.

"What if he turns out to be a maniac?" I asked.

The question was half a joke.

"That's why you're staying in a public place with him," Catherine said. "Hey, look. If you're that worried, I'll get dressed and shadow your date. No problem. I'll put on a scarf and sunglasses and sit nearby."

"Sunglasses at night?"

"Yes. Have you never seen people wearing sunglasses at night? You know, driving with sunglasses at night is illegal in most states, but some of them actually let you look cool at night while driving."

"Right. Okay, well. No need to eavesdrop on my date. In case I embarrass myself, I would rather take my chances and have Darren be a maniac who'll end up killing me than to have you know what a fool I made of myself on a date," I said.

Catherine didn't laugh. She was already used to my corny humor, but I hoped it would at least be able to evoke a smile out of Darren – if I managed to muster enough confidence to make a joke.

"You'll do fine, sweetie. It's perfectly normal to be nervous. You haven't been out on a date since forever." Catherine gave my shoulder a gentle rub and returned to the couch.

She was right. Ever since Alex, I hadn't gone out on a single date. Not even with him. I didn't even know how these things worked anymore. Has anything changed in the past few years? Any new trends or codes of conduct I needed to follow? Would Darren think badly of me for it?

You're overthinking it, I reminded myself for the millionth time that day.

"Goodbye." I waved to Catherine as I strode toward the door.

"Bye-bye, Mel. If he gets too touchy with you, let me know. I'll be there in minutes, in my pajamas and all, to kick him in the nuts."

That somehow made me feel better. Like when a parent tells their kid they'll check the closet and under the bed before bedtime for any hidden monsters. With that, I left the apartment.

DATE BITE

The closer I got to the rendezvous point, the colder it somehow got. It honestly wasn't chilly according to the weather forecast, so it must have been my anxiety creating an icy cold that penetrated to my bones.

When I reached the restaurant where Darren and I agreed to meet, he was already there, which only further exacerbated my nervousness. He hadn't seen me yet, so I took a moment to compose myself.

I closed my eyes and took deep breaths in and out to stave off the feverish shivering of my extremities. In my head, Catherine gave me a pat on the back.

You got this. You're going to do great. He's going to love you. He'll go crazy for you. You're a star, she kept saying in my head.

It sounded more like an overbearing agent giving his singer a motivational talk before a big performance. Strangely, I think it actually worked for me.

The anxiety went down a little bit, but when I peeked at Darren standing in front of the restaurant, looking all confident, a calm expression on his face, his hands in his pockets, entrenched in one spot, I felt the shivers returning.

It came on and off in intervals and more and more questions arose in my mind. *What if I slip and fall in front of him? What if I say something stupid? What if he turns out to be a sexual offender?*

I then reminded myself that those were irrational worries, just like my therapist said.

You're an overthinker, Melanie, she said. *That means that after coming to a normal conclusion about possible and normal outcomes, you continue thinking and then pile on a bunch of irrational worries. For example, it's perfectly normal to worry that your presentation might not go as you expect it to. You might stutter, forget what you wanted to say, etcetera. But it's irrational to worry about whether the ceiling will collapse and knock you out, or that you'll get fired because of the presentation, and so on.*

She was right. I mean, sure, it wasn't irrational to think I might not slip and fall – I'm kind of a klutz – but even if I did, so what? If the roles were reversed and it was Darren who slipped and fell, I wouldn't laugh at him or think about it for the rest of the date.

Before my thoughts could give me more than I'm able to handle, I stepped out in front of Darren and flashed him the most confident grin I could conjure up. I hoped it didn't look creepy.

When our eyes met, he smiled at me.

What should I go for? A handshake? A hug? Just say hi?

He relieved me of that worry when he put out his hand for a handshake. I took it, hoping he wouldn't be able to notice how much it trembled. Thank goodness for the cold because it completely eliminated the clamminess that probably would have entirely coated my palm otherwise.

"Wow, you look beautiful," Darren said.

"Oh, thank you," I said, trying to suppress a giggle.

It'd been so long since anyone called me beautiful that I clung to the compliment like a koala to a tree. It wasn't right, I thought, to feel so flattered by such a simple compliment, especially if it wasn't genuine –I hoped it was. That's what years in a toxic relationship did to you.

Darren and I went inside the restaurant. For the first few minutes, the conversation between us felt stilted, but I think that was entirely my fault. I was so nervous that I barely responded to his remarks and he was visibly trying to kill the dead air between us.

It was so strange how I could talk to him so normally all the months prior to our date that I'd known him while we were just friends. Yes, I liked him for a while, but I didn't think there was a snowball's chance in hell he'd want to ask me out.

Then at one point, he mentioned that he was single and I started seeing some signs of him liking me. Subtle signs, just enough for me to wonder whether it was all in my head or he actually liked me.

You already know how it goes after that. I started romanticizing about him during the quiet hours – just thinking about him at first, replaying our conversations in my head. Before I realized it, my mind wandered in the direction of imagining holding his hand, touching his lips, lying in bed with him, and so on.

Catherine kept telling me that he was into me and that it was obvious, but I didn't believe her. I wanted to, but a part of me remained skeptical about the whole thing. I always worried about ending up like Maria from high school who had a cruel prank played on her.

Someone told her that the captain of the football team, Roger, was into her and wanted to meet up at the park after school. She went there and instead, the entire football team showed up and made fun of her for being so gullible – even Roger himself was in on the whole thing.

Maria ran off crying and ended up changing schools after that.

A part of me believed the entire time, even during the date with Darren, that I would end up like Maria. I had to remind myself that those were the irrational thoughts. This wasn't high school anymore.

After the first few minutes of breaking the ice, speaking to Darren became easier. He did a really good job of making me feel comfortable and I realized early on that talking to him now that we were on a date was no different than how we talked before.

Pretty soon, our tongues unrolled and we were talking over each other. I hadn't even realized that over two hours had gone by. I checked my phone once to see a message from Catherine asking if I was okay.

I sent her an aloof response and continued focusing on my date. After the restaurant, Darren and I went on a walk in a nearby park. I told him everything about Alex. I didn't want to, especially because I found it rude to talk about exes on the first date, but I accidentally blurted something out and then he asked if it was okay to know more about it.

I told him how Alex and I started dating in college, how I was inexperienced and had no idea how relationships functioned, how we clung to the safety we had in the relationship even though the love was already long gone, how he was cold all the time, etc.

You'd think that he was the one who broke up with me, but no. Alex never was a self-starter, and despite being visibly miserable in the relationship, he hadn't planned on breaking up. That meant it was up to me to do it, and it was the most difficult thing I ever had to do.

Even though you no longer love a person, you're used to them being with you all day every day for the past few years. So, when that person is suddenly out of your life, there's a massive void that just refuses to go away for a long time.

I couldn't get out of bed for a whole week after ending things with Alex, but then I slowly started to rejuvenate and feel like new doors were opening to me. I also started to see just how toxic our relationship had been. That's how it always goes with relationships. You don't see the bad stuff until it's over.

Equally, if you're the one who gets dumped, you usually don't see the good stuff until then. Although I had a lot of good stuff with Alex, the negative points far outweighed the positive ones.

I had realized that I spent way too long talking to Darren about my ex. The only reason why I knew it, was because we made an entire lap around the park – and it's a big lap. I gasped and apologized, and he assured me it was totally okay.

It was getting kind of late and I knew I should head back home. As much as I wanted to kiss him, I wasn't sure if he wanted the same thing and I sure as hell wouldn't be the one to take the first step because I was too much of a coward.

"Let me walk you home," Darren said.

On our way out of the park, a stray dog appeared on the trail. The park had been completely empty and this dog was the first living creature that we've seen. It was mangy, but even through the messy fur, ribs visibly stuck out like a xylophone. The dog looked timid and confused with the way its head lowered and snapped in random directions.

"Poor thing. I wonder if it belongs to someone," I said. I squatted down outstretched my hand to beckon the dog. "Come on, pup. Come here."

"Maybe you shouldn't pet him. He, uh… he might be dangerous," Darren said.

The tentative manner in which Darren said it, almost sounded like he wasn't very fond of dogs. We had never talked about animals before, and if he didn't like dogs, he would lose points with me.

"It's okay. I can tell when dogs will bite," I said.

The dog lowered his head as it approached me. Its tail wagged left and right in such fervent wipes that its rear shook along with it. I carefully put out a hand and touched the dogs head. Its fur was crusted with something hard. I had to be gentle not to accidentally tear the poor thing's fur.

"You're a good boy, aren't you?" I asked in a sing-song voice.

I didn't even know what gender the dog was because I hadn't bothered to look between its legs, but I usually assumed the dog's gender based on the breed. Pitbulls and Poodles were females, Dobermans and Golden Retrievers were male, etc.

"Uh, be careful, Melanie. There's, uh, there's foam at his mouth," Darren tentatively said.

Sure enough, I saw white bubbles forming around the sides of the dog's mouth. I wondered if it was having some respiratory problems or anything like that. The fur around the torso also seemed sticky with something dark that reminded of blood. Was the animal hurt?

"Come on. We should head back," Darren urged, only further causing an irritation to swirl inside me.

Why couldn't he see that this dog meant no harm? It was wagging its tail, for Christ's sake. That meant it was happy. But Darren was right. We needed to go.

"So long, pup," I said as I scratched the top of its head.

It all happened so fast.

There wasn't even a warning sign. The dog's jaw opened and closed around my wrist with lightning speed with a vicious growl. The foam around its snout intensified. Its eyes suddenly took on a bloodshot appearance, just for a split second before I yelped, and the dog turned around and ran off into the darkness off the trail.

"Shit! Are you okay?!" Darren ran up to me.

I hadn't realized how far he'd been standing from me the entire time until then, only confirming my suspicion that he was apprehensive of the dog.

Rightly so, the voice in my head said. *Stray dogs. Check. Added to the anxiety list.*

I looked down at my burning wrist. The distinct bite mark coated it, enough to draw blood – not too terribly, but I would need to go to the doctor for some shots of whatever. Dammit, what an inconvenience.

Guess my irrational fears weren't so irrational after all. I then remembered that I had no one to blame but myself for approaching stray dogs. Catherine warned me a million times, but I didn't listen.

You never know how they might react, Melanie. They're unpredictable, she always said, but I always dismissed her.

They're dogs, and dogs are nice, I said. *Besides, you'll see the signs of them being aggressive.*

Well, guess I was dead wrong on that one.

"We should get you to a doctor," Darren said.

"No, no. It's okay. It's fine," I said, suppressing the tears and trying to stabilize my quavering voice.

I felt so offended. I patted that dog and he bit me. That hurt my feelings more than most of the things Alex said or did.

"You might get a disease or something," Darren said.

"I know, I know. I'll go to the doctor in the morning. It's kind of late now," I said.

It was the truth. It was almost midnight and I didn't know of any nearby ambulances that worked for things like these. Darren raised an eyebrow, ogling me in a suspicious manner.

"I promise," I said.

He looked like he still didn't believe me, but he smiled and nodded. The air between us was somewhat awkward after that. I felt like such a moron for getting bitten on our first date. It was as if the universe was giving me the middle finger, stopping me from having a good date.

No one to blame but yourself, Melanie, the jeering voice in my head said.

I tried not to make a big deal out of the bite and made small talk with Darren. The stinging sensation in the bite was distracting, but not terrible. I would put some alcohol on it once I was home, and I'd go to the doctor in the morning. I had the day off from work anyway.

When it was time for Darren and me to say goodbye, he asked me once more if my arm hurt from the bite. I appreciated his concern, but it was a little overbearing, so it also irritated me. I flashed him a grin and assured him everything was okay, that I didn't even feel any pain.

The cold actually helped numb the pain a little bit, but the sensation was still highly unpleasant. The last time I had an open wound must have been about fifteen years ago when I was still a kid and scraped my knee by falling off my bike.

Darren hugged me and said he would call me these days. I wondered if that was his way of saying "don't expect my call." I tried not to think about it too much.

LAB PART 2

"Simmons, is that what I think it is?" Phillip asked.

"Yes. It is," Simmons brusquely responded. "It is the PT-104."

"I thought all the tests for it had failed."

Phillip's hands were trembling even as he pressed them firmly into his pockets. His heart was relentlessly racing. His mind refused to believe what Doctor Simmons said was true.

"PT-104..." Phillip repeated, as if tasting the words and letting them slosh in his mouth for a moment.

He took a step closer toward the thick glass that separated the subjects' room from the observation room. The tips of his shoes smacked the wall, warning him that he was as close as he could possibly get, but it still wasn't enough for him to take a close enough look.

The room was a spacious, white chamber with a tiny table in the middle. The table, too, was white, and looking at it hurt Phillip's eyes for a little bit upon entering. The scintillating lights that reflected the white surfaces didn't help much, either.

In the middle of the table was a glass box, and inside the glass box, a petri dish. Of course, Phillip had known right away what experiment he was staring at, the moment he walked into the room. He recognized it from the big PT letters plastered to the glass box, even though he couldn't see the numbers – the company had only one organism labeled PT that they worked with.

"I thought this experiment was supposed to be scrapped," Phillip said, and only just then became aware of how constricted his throat was.

"Indeed, it was." Simmons nodded. "But I convinced the guys up top to extend the deadline for another month. They weren't happy spending extra funds on a project they considered a loss for another thirty days, but after presenting to them that we could–"

"Please spare me the irrelevant details, Simmons. Get to the meat and potatoes," Phillip interrupted.

Simmons looked offended for a moment. He cleared his throat and began anew.

"We changed the solution given to the PT-104. It's evident that the one given prior to this one hasn't worked and the organism continued rejecting it. But the newest concoction…" Simmons tented his fingers, his voice growing more and more laced with utter fascination. "The organism adopted it, consumed it. It helped it grow to much greater heights and it even allowed it to *mutate*."

"Mutate? How?"

"Come with me."

Simmons walked Phillip to the research room. Up until the moment the glass pane with the PT-104 was out of sight, Phillip held his gaze trained on the specimen. As they entered the research room, Phillip was greeted by a team of people wearing lab coats, gloves, and goggles. They were split in pairs and each team working on their own thing at the wide, pristine desks.

"Good evening, Doctor Curtis," some of them said with a hint of utter respect.

Phillip gave them a brief nod. Simmons led him past the experimentation desks toward one of the scientists who was fiddling with a microscope.

"Doctor Curtis," the scientist said with a nod, prying his gaze away from the microscope.

"Would you mind letting Doctor Curtis take a look at the specimen, Brian?" Simmons asked.

"Not at all. Go right ahead, Doctor," Brian stepped aside and gestured toward the microscope.

Phillip approached the microscope and leaned to take a look. He adjusted the zoom level until it was no longer blurry. He gasped. The tiny, blurry thing came into focus and Phillip's eyes fell on a worm-like shape. It coiled around itself and slithered in random directions, vigorously and full of energy, unlike anything he'd ever seen before.

Phillip leaned back, scratched his cheek, and then took another look. The worm was still there, this time accompanied by another, shorter one.

"My God," Phillip said as he unglued his gaze from the microscope. "It's actually thriving."

When he looked at Doctor Simmons, the man had a proud smile on his face. Phillip thought he detected something else there, too. Spite, maybe? As much as Phillip hated to admit it, Simmons was right to be spiteful toward him right now.

When the experiment first started, everything was going well, but then the PT-104 refused to react to anything. Phillip was one of the first people to call the experiment a failure and urge the higher-ups to scrap it. Simmons was adamantly against it, but since he was Phillip's subordinate, he didn't have a say in the matter.

The higher-ups ended up giving the science team a deadline before killing the funds for the project. Phillip had all but given up on the experiment and focused on the other one they'd been given.

Until tonight.

What Simmons managed to do here was impressive, to say the least. It also meant that he went behind Phillip's back and worked overtime to try and save the experiment. Hell, he even talked to the committee behind Phillip's back.

Can you blame him? If he asked you, you would have said no.

As exuberant as Phillip was to have the experiment back from the dead, he couldn't help but feel a twinge of hurt. It was his manly pride that suffered, he knew. He didn't want to let it get in the way, though. Something far greater than him and his manhood was at stake and he had to use the momentum to further develop the experiment.

"All right, Doctor Simmons. Fill me in," Phillip said.

"Follow me." Simmons gestured with his head toward the corridor leading to the rest of the subject rooms.

"We've already tested the PT-104 on some live specimens."

"And it worked this time?"

"Remarkably, yes. When we first tested it, the parasite had no effect on any living creature."

"Except the *theraphosa blondi*," Phillip added.

"The goliath birdeater tarantula, yes. The PT-104 was only able to thrive in the body of the arachnid, and no matter how much we tried, we couldn't get it to integrate itself into anything else," Simmons said.

Phillip had spent countless hours of overtime trying to make the PT-104 work. He forced Simmons and the rest of the team to work so hard that they literally ended up collapsing on their feet from exhaustion – all so he could create something new, something magnificent.

26

But the harder they tried, the harder they failed. The PT-104 refused to live in any other organism, including humans, and died within hours of getting injected. For Simmons to find a solution was nothing short of impressive.

Simmons stopped in front of one of the subject rooms – it was a small cell-like room, but instead of bars, a protective, bulletproof glass stood as a barrier. The room was empty. That was where patient zero had been tested on – Lola, the rabbit. It seemed like a lifetime ago.

"Well, now we've finally managed to mutate the PT-104 to have it adapt to a life in *any* organism," Simmons said.

"What do you mean by *any*?"

"Exactly that, Doctor Curtis. *Any* organism. Rats, mice, pigs, bears, unicorns, you name it."

"What about…"

"Humans?"

A sadistic smile stretched across Simmons' face at that question. He stopped in front of the subject room labeled with a large number 3 above. Phillip looked through the glass. At first, it appeared as though the room was empty.

Messy, but empty.

But then among the mess, his gaze fell on what Doctor Simmons so badly wanted him to see.

AFTERMATH

When I returned home, Catherine was still up, still cooped up in her blankets, in the same position where she was when I left, like a plant rooted to one spot. As soon as she heard the door opening, her head snapped in my direction, eyes beaming with anticipation and excitement.

"Well?!" she asked, almost breathless.

"I think it went okay," I said.

That's what I honestly thought.

"What do you mean, *okay*?" Catherine asked and then scooted to the side, making room for me on the couch. "Come on, tell me all about it."

I dropped my handbag on the coffee table and slumped onto the couch. I hadn't realized how exhausted I was until I felt the soft, warm furniture greeting my fall, gently, like a cloud.

Catherine had her knees up to her chin and was sitting sideways, facing me, her head propped above her palm.

"So, tell me all about it," she said, and I could tell that she was barely able to contain the excitement in her voice.

"Well..." I presented my injured wrist. "I got bitten by a dog."

The smile on Catherine's face drooped and she let out the sigh of a disappointed parent. "You're shitting me."

"I wish."

"Melanie, I told you a million times that–" Catherine threw her hands up and closed her eyes, as if to compose herself, before looking at me again. "Okay, tell me what happened."

I inhaled and exhaled deeply. Catherine's reaction only made me feel worse. Now, in the warmth of the apartment, the bite mark pulsated with a painful sensation. I excused myself to take care of it despite Catherine's protests.

I ran cold water on the wound and washed off the excess blood that had dried on my forearm. Not a big bite. Nothing terrible, honestly. My biggest worry was the infection.

Could I get rabies? It was possible, but I thought rabies was pretty much eradicated around these parts, right? I still couldn't risk it. Rabies was one of the deadliest viruses and once the incubation period was over, the chances of surviving it were quite low.

I would go to the doctor in the morning for a shot or whatever it was they gave in these situations. It would probably cost me a lot, but I should do it anyway, just in case.

Lesson learned. Shouldn't pet stray dogs no matter how amicable they look.

I bandaged my wrist, even though it wasn't bleeding. I just didn't want the wound getting infected, if it wasn't already. I returned to the living room and told Catherine all about my date, including the dog bite.

During the story, I expected her to burst into a laughing fit, but that never happened. She leered at me with that stare of a parent, and it only made me feel worse. Hearing her laugh would give me some assurance that it was no big deal – a matter to be laughed at. But the serious expression on her face told me that the bite and my talk about Alex might have some dire consequences on my date.

"Well, the important thing is that the date went well," Catherine finally said as she clambered up to her feet and sauntered to the kitchen.

"Yeah, I think it did," I said.

"What do you mean, you think? You said it yourself. You were both talkative. He showed signs of liking you." Catherine opened the fridge and leaned into it, the door shielding her from my view.

I heard rummaging coming from it, and a moment later, she straightened her back and closed the door shut, a can of caramel chocolate ice cream in her hand. She opened one of the drawers and I heard metallic clattering. She closed it and was on her way back to the couch, the ice cream and two spoons in her hands.

"Whoa, I can't eat that," I said, my palm reflexively raised in a stop sign.

"You had a good date. It needs to be celebrated," Catherine said as she took her spot on the couch.

She handed me one spoon. I took it without thinking while she removed the lid on the ice cream.

"I don't really know if it went that well," I said.

"Sure, it did. I told you, Darren likes you. Like, a lot."

"You really think so?" I asked, even though I already knew the answer.

I guess I just needed some assurance after the whole dog bite incident. Just then, a loud ping came from the coffee table. It took me a moment to realize it was my phone.

"See?" Catherine said. "Wanna bet that's your boyfriend?"

I blushed. *Your boyfriend.* Hearing Darren being referred to as my boyfriend brought butterflies to my stomach. I eagerly reached for my handbag and dug out the mobile phone. I fully expected the message to be from my cellphone provider or spam mail.

Sure enough, Catherine was right. It was from Darren.

Hey. I had a really good time with you tonight, Melanie. I hope we can do this again soon. Please make sure to take care of that bite.

I only became aware of the smile on my face once Catherine's booming voice snapped me back to reality.

"See? What did I tell you? You have him wrapped around your little finger." She made a show of rotating her little finger in tiny circles.

"I do not. I would never want to do that," I said as I started typing a response to Darren.

"Why not?" Catherine asked.

"Because it's evil."

"So what? It's okay to do it sometimes."

"Like when?"

"Like when you guys are getting to know each other and you want the turn the odds in your favor." Catherine shrugged. "Guys do it all the time, too. They lie and manipulate. One time, I've even had a guy I liked hire a woman to pretend to be his girlfriend just to see if I would get jealous."

"Darren's not like that. He's really sweet and kind. Right?" I turned to face her, averting my gaze from the half-finished text.

"Yeah. He is. He's never cheated on any of his girlfriends as far as I know. And he was always a real gentleman. Come to think of it, some girls left him because he's too nice, you know?"

"Because he's too nice?" I echoed.

"Yeah. I guess they saw that as a weakness or something."

"Their loss." I continued typing the message.

Thank you so much for taking me out. I had a lot of fun, too. I hope to see you again soon!

The last sentence was initially written as *I can't wait to see you again,* but then I realized it may be a little too much after the first date, so I changed it. I then added, *Oh, and don't worry about the dog. It's just a small bite.*

"Well, at least you can sue the city now for having a stray dog bite you," Catherine said.

"Eh, too much hassle. And not enough cash for it."

"It could at least cover your medical expenses."

I pondered that for a moment, but ultimately decided that it would still be too much hassle finding a lawyer, pressing charges, proving that I was bitten, only to get just enough cash to cover the healthcare bill, and maybe not even that much.

"It's no big deal," I said nonchalantly. "I'll go to the doctor in the morning. It's just a small bite, anyway."

I went to bed but couldn't fall asleep for at least two hours because my brain raced a million thoughts an hour. I replayed the date with Darren in my head, allowing the butterflies in the stomach to fly while I enjoyed the sensation.

I swear to God, when I first had that feeling with Darren, I thought I was coming down with something. Now, I enjoyed the feeling of weakness it gave me. As I drifted into sleep, I could vividly imagine kissing Darren. It felt so real that I swear I could feel the soft touch of his lips on mine.

The dreamy state was interrupted by a growling, wrinkled snout of a mangy dog that lunged at my face, its teeth ready to sink into my skin. I awoke with a start, covered in cold sweat. The bite wound pulsated more intensely.

I ignored it and went back to sleep.

HOSPITAL

I completely forgot about everything that transpired the night before when I woke up. That is, until I accidentally pressed my palm into the bedsheets and felt the searing pain that jolted through it.

I hissed and grabbed at my painful wrist. I expected to see blood seeping through the bandages, like when the hero of the movie suffers a gunshot, pulls out the bullet and bandages the injury, shrugging off the "minor" wound before continuing to put holes in the hordes of enemies that awaited him.

Considering how much I winced at the bite mark – which wasn't even that deep, by the way – I figured I would not make a great movie hero. As much as I wanted to unwrap the bandage and see what the injury looked like, I refrained from doing so because I'd be going to the doctor in a bit anyway.

Getting an appointment scheduled was no problem. They had a last-minute cancelation and were able to take me in. I usually didn't start work until ten or eleven – lazy, I know – because I worked as a software engineer. That meant that if I had no meetings, which I usually didn't, I could work whenever I wanted and however long I wanted, as long as I met the project's deadline.

Catherine was already gone by the time I woke up and I remembered that she had some kind of an early meeting with partners based in the UK. She, too, was a software engineer, but she worked for a different company. That was probably why we became such good friends.

When I first moved to Seattle looking for an apartment, I knew I couldn't afford something too pricy. The three-bedroom apartment in Arbor Heights stole my heart at first glance, but I knew I couldn't afford to live in it alone.

Luckily, the landlord mentioned that he was okay with multiple people living in the apartment if it would make it easier for me and he gave me Catherine's number, mentioning that she was another girl interested in renting.

I texted Catherine asking if she wanted to meet up – I freaking hated calling – but she ended up giving me a call. I reluctantly answered and we agreed to meet up. Neither of us wanted to admit it, but the only reason why we decided to see each other was because we wanted to gauge if we would be able to live with the other person as a roommate.

It's safe to say that we hit it off really well immediately. Once we learned that we were both starting work as engineers, opening up was easy. I'm usually not talkative, but with Catherine, it was natural. We didn't just have the same jobs. We had other things in common, like things we liked, things we hated, routines, food tastes, and similar.

We met up with the landlord the same day and got the apartment.

I took an apple and ate it on the way out of the apartment, since I wouldn't have time for breakfast. On the elevator ride down, Mrs. Dawson from the apartment next door mentioned how she heard me coming home late last night.

How she heard that was beyond me, but she'd proven multiple times that she had a keen eye and ear when it came to sticking her nose in other people's business. She proceeded to tell me how a young woman like me should know better than to go fooling around so late, further mentioning that only the bad kind of folk were out during that time.

She was trying to allude to me being a prostitute, but I didn't fall for the bait. I listened to everything with a rictus through the agonizing ride down that lasted just long enough for me to wish I took the stairs.

When the doors finally opened, I dismissively thanked her and loped out of the building, leaving her to continue rambling to herself as if I were still there.

The traffic was bad, but it was like this every morning – something I needed time to get used to once I moved to Seattle. I was irritated, which said a lot about me, because I rarely felt that way.

I mean, you'd have to really push my buttons to get my anger to actually manifest. I was pretty good at bottling it up – something my therapist says was a bad idea – so if my anger somehow showed, it meant I was really pissed.

That morning, it showed when a swear word left my mouth and I honked to the driver in front of me who blocked the intersection. I couldn't remember what the swear word was because I uttered it in the heat of the moment, but I knew that only later I vaguely registered saying it.

I was kind of hoping for a slow drive to the doctor because I wanted to reminisce my date with Darren. The crazy drivers of Seattle made that daydreaming impossible. I think the pulsating in my wrist also made me extra irritable.

As much as I wanted to blame the dog, I couldn't. It was probably scared, sick, might have been abused in the past, as well. It was just an animal acting on its instinct. I couldn't blame it for that no more than I could a pack of lions for killing a gazelle to feed its babies.

The doctor's office was particularly empty, which was odd because this clinic was always packed.

I didn't complain. Getting into the office sooner also meant being able to start working sooner. I estimated that I could start working at nine, which meant I'd finish one hour earlier.

When I first got the job, my intention was to wake up at six so I could start working at seven and finish by three. The thought of having the entire afternoon free seemed so heavenly.

Unfortunately, that's not how the corporate world worked. Most of the working people decided last minute that they needed something, so they scheduled meetings at 4 or 5 P.M. That meant that even if I finished work earlier, I would need to log in from my laptop to attend the meeting or at least read the minutes.

Also, I'm not an early bird. I mean, I can be, but only for a while. Back before I started working, I had this phase where I woke up at 4 A.M. to go to the gym and started my day fresh and early. Unfortunately, the lack of sleep accumulated over time and I crashed.

I felt best when I went to bed before midnight and slept until 9 A.M.

Doctor Howard Mills remembered me from the last time when I visited because of a finger I thought was broken. Spoiler alert – it wasn't. It did give me quite a scare, though, so I have been careful about how I handled heavy objects ever since.

"Melanie, back so soon?" Dr. Mills asked with a lopsided smile.

"Believe me, I would love nothing more than to never see you again in my life… at least not in your scrubs. But it is what it is. Oh, that reminds me, I ate an apple today. I hope that doesn't kill you or something."

The doctor laughed at my stupid joke. I didn't care whether it was courtesy or not – I personally was proud of my sense of humor.

"So, what seems to be the problem?" he asked.

"Well, I, uh… I went out on a date yesterday and I thought it would be a good idea to pet a stray dog. It, uh, it bit me. So…"

"Ouch." The doctor made a sour grimace. "Well, let's take a look."

I was about to unwrap the bandage, but the doctor did it for me. The fabric stuck to the wound and unsticking it caused me to wince in pain. I should have put some gauze there, I figured way too late.

The doctor made small talk with me while taking care of my wound. It helped take my mind off the pain and anxiety that accumulated when he prepared the bandages and dressings he planned on putting on my wound.

He said that it'd been infected, but treating it would be no problem. He also gave me some shots and antibiotics and told me how to take them. He was so nice and it made the whole visit more pleasant than expected.

Usually, when I visit a doctor's office, I feel uncomfortable and want to get it over with as soon as possible. It must have something to do with the distinct medicinal smell pervading the air, the staff in scrubs ambling down the corridors with a sense of urgency, the other patients in the waiting room with downcast facial expressions….

But this clinic was incongruously different than what I got used to. The staff here were overwhelmingly friendly, and the place was actually nicely decorated with plants and artwork, rather than having nothing but pure white hallways.

That feeling of being welcome and treated so nicely plummeted once I saw the bill. I had to remind myself once more that this was an unnecessary cost that could have been avoided if only I hadn't pet the dog.

I would just need to avoid petting stray animals from here on out. I didn't like the idea of lonely dogs that actually deserved attention to go unnoticed by me on the streets, but I wouldn't be able to afford another visit to the doctor, so… sorry, dogs.

Work went by as it usually does. I had started to feel a little overwhelmed with all the bug-solving requests until I received a message from Darren. Immediately, my mood soared from despondent to buoyant.

Him sending me a message confirmed for me that the date went well. I knew it probably should have been obvious, but like I said, I was kind of paranoid when it came to those things. We agreed to meet again in two weeks, as soon as he came back from his business trip to South Carolina.

I was tempted to ask him to meet tonight before his flight, but I didn't want to come off as needy. I would be patient and once he was back, we would meet up. I would continue texting him until then, continue to build our relationship a little bit.

On my way home, I ran into a pack of stray dogs. They seemed good-natured enough, but I wasn't going to take my chances – even though I really wanted to. In fact, I was about to beckon them over but the bandage on my wrist that peeked out of my sleeve reminded me not to do it.

I could almost imagine a pair of scornful eyes drawn on the fabric scowling at me, judging me with their penetrating glower.

Hasn't one medical bill been enough, Mel? Do you really love splurging money so much?

Instead, I went straight home, took my meds, and watched a movie with Catherine.

She wasn't very talkative that evening because she had a bad day at work – at her company, a bad day at work was, and I paraphrase, dealing with morons and idiots who couldn't even wipe their own asses.

The work-life balance was definitely a lot more messed up for Catherine. Her company was a lot more fast-paced and required much better organization of time, whereas mine was slow and relaxed.

That was why she had much better benefits than me – free food and snacks throughout the entire day, electronics dispensers in case you were missing a piece of equipment to work, big offices with bean bags, comfortable chairs, and large screens on the wall you could book all for yourself, gaming rooms, napping rooms, free bike service, a company gym, and more.

By the way, if your company has similar benefits, it's because they want to make you as comfortable as they can so you would stay longer hours in the office. I'm not complaining about those things, mind you. I love them.

I just didn't believe companies were doing it because they cared about employees – I was convinced they were doing it because they knew that the competition for finding good software engineers was rough.

Take my company, for example. They offer similar benefits to Catherine's, but they also enforce frequent team building in the form of laser tag, escape rooms, and so on. Honestly, those kinds of things can be overwhelming at times.

It's hard enough to get any work done with all the meetings, but being surrounded by such overly friendly co-workers while not being able to reciprocate the gestures can take its toll.

Anyway, whenever Catherine has a bad day at work, I can tell right away because she's quiet and her face is rigid. I'm okay with that. All I need to do on those days is leave her alone – don't make small talk, don't ask any questions – not even to check what she wants for dinner.

As someone who has shared a dorm room with a girl who used to lash out at the tiniest inconveniences, I found Catherine's bouts of bad mood a blessing.

My wrist was on fire that night, more so than last night, so I decided to call it a night and go to bed earlier.

LAB PART 3

Phillip couldn't utter a word for a moment. A human test subject was inside the room, a woman in her early twenties. From what Phillip could see, she had blonde hair and blue eyes, was slim, and despite the stress that coated her face, she was beautiful.

She had been huddled on the bed when Phillip and Simmons stopped in front of her. When they stopped in front of her room, her head snapped in their direction. She hopped up to her feet and rushed toward the glass.

The first time a subject had done that, Phillip flinched. Now, he remained rock-still, even as the woman slammed into the glass and pounded on it with her palms.

No sound came from the room, not even a squeak. The woman relentlessly smacked the glass over and over, her mouth contorting into various words that Phillip couldn't read, panic and indignation lacing her face.

No, there was one sentence Phillip managed to read among the imperceptible mouth shapes that she made.

Please let me out.

"I'm surprised you managed to find a subject on such short notice," Phillip said.

"Finding test subjects is never a problem. I forgot what her name is, but she ran away from home when she was sixteen because her parents put too much pressure on her, then met the wrong guy and started doing drugs. Her parents called the police to have her arrested when she was eighteen and they caught her stealing from their home at night. After getting released from juvie, she spent the rest of her life living on the streets. Her parents had died in a tragic car accident in the meantime and left her with nothing. No one will miss her."

The woman relentlessly pounded on the glass, uttering the same words of plea. Phillip thought he also saw her face morphing into anger. It would dissipate soon, and once the doctors left her sight, she would huddle into a fetal position and cry until she passed out. Her life would revolve around sleeping, eating, getting tests done by scientists, rinse and repeat – until she expired.

"She's been injected with the PT-104, I take it?" Phillip asked.

"Yes. Just a few hours ago," Simmons nodded.

"Do we know anything about the incubation period?"

"It's… still volatile. The parasite can develop rather fast, but many factors need to be considered for an accurate estimation."

"Such as temperature, the subject's age and gender, etcetera. Yes, we already know that. Do you have a ballpark figure?"

Simmons assumed a pensive gaze as he looked at the subject. The woman's mouth was wide open, the veins on her neck bulging. Phillip was grateful for being unable to hear her screaming.

"It can vary. The longest we've had for it to develop in someone was two weeks," Simmons said.

"And the shortest?"

"Four days."

Phillip gasped through his teeth. That sounded like it was incredibly fast. If the PT-104 got into the wrong hands, it could be the end of civilization as they knew it. Phillip had only once thought about the enormity of such a situation, and that was when he started working for the company.

He spent the first two weeks worrying about whether he would carry, the virus he was working on out with him, and infect his wife and daughter, and then the entire world. It wracked him so much that he had consistent nightmares about the world lying in ruins because of him.

After a while, he grew desensitized to it. Working with a deadly microorganism was just his daily job, nothing more. Once he hung the lab coat up on the wall, he was Phillip Curtis, the family man who watched football, took his daughter to ballet lessons, and occasionally cooked lunch for his family.

"Guide me through the stages," Phillip said to Simmons.

Simmons nodded. "I will. But I have to warn you, it won't be pretty."

FIRST STAGE

The week went by without a hitch. The bite mark on my wrist had pretty much healed, leaving a small scab. I had almost forgotten about it completely until five days after the bite.

It was morning and I was getting ready for work. Catherine was still at home. She had made eggs and coffee for us. She was under no obligation to make breakfast for the both of us since we had agreed to swap between each other cooking dinner only – we had lunch at the company most of the days and ordered takeout on the weekends.

"So, how are things with you and Darren?" she asked as she stuffed a forkful of eggs in her mouth.

"Good." I nodded. "We text every day. He hates South Carolina."

"I think he generally dislikes anything south."

"Yeah. He says they might prolong his business trip for another four or five days. He's pissed about it."

"Hm." Catherine said as she gulped down the eggs. "They often do that to him."

"Prolong his trip, you mean?" I asked.

"Not just that. But also choose him for the trip, even though there are other people who are doing nothing but standing with their dicks in their hands."

I shook my head. I wondered whether Darren thought about changing jobs. He never expressed contempt for his current job, but maybe he was just trying not to sound too negative in front of me. I took a mental note to ask him about it as soon as we go out on our next date.

"Oh, I almost forgot to tell you–" Catherine started, her hand reaching across the counter and touching my wrist.

"Ow!" I winced, sharp pain surging through my forearm as if she had just pinched a nerve there.

Catherine's hand pulled back with a jerk as if burned, concern lacing her face.

"What's wrong? What did I do?" she asked.

I pulled back the sleeve covering my wrist. Even doing that was painful. The nerves in my forearm were on fire all the way up to the knuckles from how Catherine touched me.

Supinating my wrist left and right, I observed the bite mark. The imprint of teeth was barely discernible now, only a small scab adorning my arm. I looked for any signs of bloating, pus, or something that might indicate an infection – according to the internet, of course, because I'm no medical expert.

It looked okay, but the skin was really tender to the touch. I flexed my fingers a few times, waiting for the pain to subside.

"Does it hurt?" Catherine asked with a concerned inflection.

"Yeah. I guess it hasn't healed yet."

"Maybe you should call the doc."

"No, it's fine. He already gave me meds for it, so nothing more he can do. Anyway, I should get going to work. I do want to hear that story tonight, though, all right?"

"You got it."

I left for work and honestly forgot all about the bite mark until the next time I accidentally brushed it against the side of the table and sent the same kind of pain through my arm.

Okay, so no problem. I would just need to be more careful with how I used my arm. But instead of allaying, the pain only increased.

It had started to become bothersome, to be honest. When I first got bitten, the injury burned, but it wasn't as obtrusive as it was a week later. Every accidental touch, scratch, swipe, or anything else that came in contact with the scab, sent a jolt of electrical pain through my forearm.

I tried not to pay attention to it as much as I possibly could but forgetting about it, only to accidentally whack or touch it too hard, served as a constant reminder. I'd be walking down the office corridor and someone from the other department who was in the rush would snag my wrist with the edge of their handbag or suitcase and I would spend an entire minute writhing in pain until it subsided.

Since the pain didn't seem to be going away and instead got worse with each passing day, I called the doctor again. I had finished taking the antibiotics by then.

The doctor asked me to send him a picture of the injury so he could assess if the infection was still there. I did as he asked, and after checking it out, he confirmed that it was okay and that I probably just needed some time to have it heal fully.

That gave me enough assurance. The pain was still here, but I was able to cope with it just a little bit better. In fact, I tried to use my hand as normally as I would without the injury.

For a while, it seemed to work, but then the pain became unbearable. One particular day, after using the arm for coding for over two hours, I was in so much pain that it became all I could focus on.

My co-workers in the meeting noticed that I was a little pale and told me I should call off all the meetings for the day. I gladly did that. I wanted to focus on just coding, but the pain in my arm was too intense.

It didn't matter.

I was way ahead of the deadline, so I could afford one day off. Like I said, my company was flexible and they let their employees work whenever they wanted as long as they did their work and completed projects on time.

I packed my things and drove back home. I chose the worst time to leave because it was a rush hour, which meant lots of honking the millisecond the light turned green, swearing out the windows, potential traffic accidents, and worse.

That day, I became one of the angry drivers. My forearm pulsated painfully, waves that intermittently came on and off, sometimes stronger, sometimes weaker, but always present.

I had developed a habit of flexing my fingers and forearm muscles just to see if the pain would still be there. It was, and despite telling myself that I was only making it worse with the contractions and should just leave it to rest, I couldn't help it.

It reminded me of Uncle Earl, who had chronic back pain, and despite that, insisted on bending down and picking up things with his spine arched as a banana. I told him not to do it because he was only making the pain worse, but he said the exercise helped him.

The last time I heard from Uncle Earl, he needed a discectomy, which he kept postponing despite the pain in his back only becoming worse and worse.

As I observed my arm, I tried to imagine what lay under the skin that was causing me so much pain. A sore muscle? Scar tissue?

The pain had actually spread from my wrist up to my hand and down toward my elbow. I was sure I had exacerbated it with my flexing and overusing. That was okay. I would rest the arm as much as I could for the next few days and everything would be back to normal.

I had to be smarter than Uncle Earl. He had the pain in his back, and it went away for a little bit, but as soon as it did, he continued doing the heavy lifting around the house, causing the pain to return.

It was better to miss out some days of work but then fully heal, rather than perpetually go on and off with chronic pain. I mean, I was sure my pain was nothing serious compared to Uncle Earl's, and that I would be ready to live my life normally, pain-free, within the next two or so weeks.

I grew to envy Uncle Earl's pain.

FEVER

I continued living life normally, minus one arm. I made a sling for my arm, isolating it from any kind of movement as much as I possibly could.

It was impossible to completely stop it from moving, though – a twitch here, a jerk there, just enough to remind me that it was still sore. Doing any kind of simple daily activities was pretty difficult. I don't think we realize how much we take it for granted having two functional limbs.

I sure did until I found myself constrained to using only one hand to open a bottle, type on a keyboard, text, squeeze the paste onto my toothbrush, and so on. But I didn't complain. I soldiered through it, determined to give my arm the rest it needed in order to get back to its full functionality.

It wasn't looking good, though. The soreness had spread further into my hand and forearm, and even the slightest contractions caused me to gasp and wince in pain. It was making me really irritable, as well, which I hadn't noticed until Catherine pointed it out.

"I am *not* irritable, what the hell are you talking about?" I asked as I elbowed the fridge door shut, a chocolate pudding in my hand.

The sling was no longer around my neck by then. Furious at the obvious fact that it wasn't helping, I had yanked it off and thrown it into a trash can on the street.

"Exactly this," Catherine said. "I've never seen you like this before. Did something happen? Did Darren do something?"

I sighed. It made me feel like shit to realize how badly I must have been behaving to Catherine.

"Sorry," I said. "It's just that this pain in my arm is really annoying. I can't do anything properly."

"Why don't you call your doctor?" Catherine asked.

"I don't want to bother him so often. He must already think I'm a hypochondriac."

"Mel, you paid for it. The least he can do is tell you if your arm is okay."

"Yeah, I guess you're right," I said as I struggled to open the pudding.

The plastic lid on top refused to come off until Catherine stepped in to help me.

"Thanks," I said as I dipped the spoon into the chocolate. "I'll wait a couple more days and then I'll call him."

"All right. Maybe you should take a few days off from work, too. All that typing must be doing no good for your arm."

"I'm not using this arm for typing," I said.

As soon as the words left my mouth, I realized how offended I must have sounded, because I was. No, not offended. Fed up.

"Oh," was all Catherine said before waltzing back to the couch. "Yeah, definitely call your doctor and see what he says."

Yikes, something's wrong with your arm and they might need to amputate it, was what it sounded more like, but I chose not to respond to that.

I ate the pudding, not caring that it wasn't proper dinner, and went to my room. I like to sleep on my stomach, with the hands tucked under the pillow. You can guess that that sleeping position was no longer an option, so I had to sleep either on the side or on my back.

The problem was, I had difficulty falling asleep on my side, and I couldn't ever fall asleep on my back. Even if I ever did, I would wake up in the middle of the night and my body was all uncomfortable, as if warning me that this wasn't the right sleeping position, not letting me drift back to dreamland until I switched to a different position.

In the morning, the pain was somewhat weaker. I honestly felt so relieved about it that I wanted to scream in happiness. Something like that shouldn't have been such a big deal, but it was for me. The pain was still present, but much less than before.

The urge to flex my hand was strong, but I resisted it. The last thing I needed was for the pain to return. I carefully retraced my steps. What could I have done that caused the pain to diminish?

The only thing I did differently was not eating as healthy as before. Maybe that was the problem – I was in a caloric deficit and it caused the pain to linger. It was, of course, natural that the body would require a long time to recover while not having a proper caloric intake, and was sure that the pudding for dinner plus the slice of pizza for lunch must have thrown me into a sufficiency instead.

If eating junk food was what helped my arm heal, then that's exactly what I would continue doing.

Reflecting on that, indeed, the junk food was the trick because every day, my arm kept getting better and better. It was still sore, but at least I could use it properly for work and other stuff.

"See? You were worried for nothing," Catherine said, making me feel like a total idiot for ever having such a meltdown over arm pain.

I impatiently texted Darren every day, eagerly awaiting his return. He bore the bad news that his trip got extended for an extra week. I was almost glad, because the ordeal made him say that he wished he could be home sooner because he missed me.

My skin prickled when I read that message. I spent a solid five or so minutes rereading the message just to make sure that I perceived it right. My brain feverishly scanned the line of text, looking for a typo or a different meaning that caused Darren to make such an egregious mistake.

But it was still there, even after reading it for the hundredth time. Darren actually missed me. The butterflies in my stomach turbulently swirled and flew in circles. Minutes later, I learned that those weren't butterflies when I felt bile climbing up to my throat.

I made it to the bathroom just in time to barf into the toilet. I have no idea what came over me. I had been feeling somewhat nauseous that whole day, but this came out of the blue. I hadn't puked since that one time when I went out with Catherine and got blackout drunk.

I had no recollection of vomiting, but Catherine swore on her life it was true, and even showed me the brown stain in the bathroom as proof. I still wasn't sure whether I believed her, though.

After shooting the first projectile into the toilet, I remained suspended above it because I felt more climbing into my throat. It was a good call because more discolored liquid riddled with undigested bits of food shot out of my mouth.

God, that must have been the worst sensation ever – knowing that the food and liquid unsteadily sloshing in your stomach would come back shooting through your mouth and you would be powerless to stop it. Whenever I puked, some of it even went through my nose, which left a lingering burning sensation in my nostrils.

Absolutely disgusting.

I had no idea how people who loved to drink could do something like this every weekend. I used to hang out with a guy from college named Hunter who absolutely lived for Friday and Saturday nights. But he wasn't one of those people who simply liked going out, dancing to loud music, and drinking until amnesia kicked in.

No, Hunter was a prodigy and an overachiever in drinking. He proudly told everyone about the time he attended an all-you-can-drink party where he got kicked out because he drank everything the house had to offer, and about the time he had to go to the hospital for stomach pumping.

Despite having such a crazy resilience to alcohol, he still managed to get utterly drunk every weekend, which caused him to get in all sorts of accidents and altercations. Every Monday, I'd see him with a new bruise or cut.

I got this one after I tried climbing a billboard. This one is from banging my head on a car window. This one, I don't personally remember, but the guys say I burned cigarettes on the skin. Pretty rad, huh?

As the years went by, his resilience wore off and I saw him more and more hungover, slurring his words, lethargic, and devoid of the life he displayed while having a bottle in his hand. He'd often mumble something about not drinking until at least the end of the month only to be seen in a club that same weekend.

Hunter worked as a sales consultant in a big company, but his weekend alter-ego still thrived.

The third projectile of puke shot through my mouth and nose into the toilet. I was panting, my breath smelling like rotten food, snot hanging from my nose, my throat burning, tiny chunks of the chicken sandwich in my mouth.

I spat and did a farmer's blow to get the snot out of my nose. The waves of vomiting were over, I thought. I remained above the toilet just to be on the safe side. A few meager burps left my mouth, but nothing more flew out, thank God.

I flushed the toilet, cleaned myself up, and my eyes shifted toward my reflection in the mirror. I looked like shit. My skin was pallid, my forehead coated with beads of sweat, dark eyebags adorning my face, my hair disheveled with the strands jutting in various directions.

Weakness overtook my body all of a sudden. My legs were wobbly, as if standing on a pair of sticks that could snap at any moment from the weight. I felt lightheaded and unstable, as if I could collapse at any moment.

I retreated to the bedroom and plopped into bed. The moment I did, it hit me just how exhausted I was. If someone threatened me with a gun at that moment to get up, I think I would have told them to just shoot me.

A shiver swaddled my entire body while my forehead incongruously burned with a raging hot temperature. I put the back of my hand on my forehead to feel how warm it was. It was impossible to tell how hot it was and I didn't have a thermometer to check my temperature.

Pretty stupid not having such a thing, I know, but I rarely come down with a fever.

In fact, me becoming sick so suddenly was a shock. I figured it wouldn't last too long because I usually got sick for a day or two and then I got better.

I asked Catherine to make me some chicken soup and tea, and buy me some vitamins. She took good care of me, and even checked up on me every hour or so. Such a good roommate. I played my fever off as it being no big deal and told her I'd try and get some sleep.

I spent the entire night tossing and turning.

LAB PART 4

The face of the blonde test subject still lingered in Phillip's mind – the way she screamed and pleaded, the way she pounded on the glass in what must have been a really painful way.

Just like working with the deadly microorganisms, Phillip felt nothing when he saw that woman.

When he first started working for the company, they warned him that the things they did were not for the faint of heart. They had taken him on an orientation where they had showed him the quarantine. The first two rooms had animal specimens – a rat and a raccoon, Phillip remembered.

But the third room had a human test subject. How the company managed to get so many live human tests subjects without raising suspicion was something Phillip still didn't understand. Not that he had tried finding out. Some things were best left well enough alone.

Phillip still clearly remembered the person's face. It was a young boy, no older than seventeen. The poor kid had been drugged so badly that he had no idea what was going on. He had been sitting in the corner of the room, his head lolling from one side to the other, his gaze wandering in random directions. He had been utterly unaware of Phillip and the orientation instructor.

The room next to that one also had a human test subject. This one was a woman in her thirties. Unlike the boy, she was very much aware of her surroundings, and

61

just like the blonde girl from the moments before, pounded on the glass and demanded to be let out.

Her features remained carved in Phillip's head for a long time.

Warts covered her from head to toe, so much that she was unrecognizable. Her face had been so densely populated with the blisters that her skin was only visible in small patches here and there. The warts had grown so badly over her left eyelid that she couldn't open it.

Some of them had been scratched open, leaking blood and white substances. Her fingers were like tree bark. When she opened her mouth to shout, Phillip saw that warts covered her tongue and the inside of her mouth, as well.

Once the orientation was over, Phillip had a one-on-one conversation with the chief of security. The conversation was more of an interrogation to gauge whether Phillip would spill the beans to the police or anyone else about what the company worked on. The chief made it very clear that Phillip would be monitored in the next couple of weeks, and if so much as tried to go to the police, there would be consequences.

He didn't say it exactly like that, of course, but Phillip knew how to read between the lines.

Phillip went on to sign the company's NDA, which he made sure to read thoroughly. It wasn't like the usual terms of agreement that one would read at the bank or when buying a car – everything written in tiny letters leaving room for ambiguity.

No, this one was riddled with red warnings and repeated words like "termination," which Phillip was sure had a more severe meaning than just losing his job.

He took his job *very* seriously from the moment he left his signature on paper. So much that he'd never even told his family what exactly it was he did at the company. For all they knew, he was a scientist working on a diet pill.

After a while of seeing those human test subjects and even working with them, Phillip no longer saw them as humans. The company made sure to refer to them all times as "test subjects" or "specimens." The scientists were also forbidden to make small talk with them, to avoid getting attached, growing a conscience, and potentially doing something stupid.

Phillip had thought he would lose his mind during the first two months of working for the company. He was sure he would snap at one point and tell the police everything before deciding to off himself. Things only became easier the longer he worked.

It's amazing how humans can adapt to almost any situation when necessary.

Now, seeing those "creatures" behind the thick pane of glass evoked no feelings whatsoever in Phillip. They were things to be used for greater purposes, not humans who could harbor feelings.

Simmons and Phillip stopped in front of a subject in the room 4. Inside the room was a pig. Phillip got closer to the glass and squinted. The pig had patches of open wounds where rot and maggots festered, eating on its flesh. The pig seemed unaware of it as it nibbled on a piece of dead meat on the ground – its own meat, Phillip realized.

"The parasite can transfer through exchange of saliva or blood, most notably, biting," Simmons said. "Infection rate is over 99 percent, which means once you're bitten by an infected animal, the chances of not becoming affected are extremely low."

"We're not doing second-grade math here, Doctor Simmons. Give me the *important* info," Phillip said.

"The parasite used to be able to thrive only in the body of the tarantula, just as we've mentioned before. Getting inserted in any other organism resulted in the parasite's death. Similarly to *toxoplasma gondii,* the parasite could survive in a human or another organism for a short while, but no patterns of change would be noted."

"Go on," Phillip said, his gaze fixated on the pig.

It threw its head back and then lowered its snout, sniffing the blood-covered floor, most likely in search of more food.

"Once the parasite is inside the host, it incubates for the time we are yet to determine. Once the incubation period is over, the parasite hatches and lays millions and millions of eggs inside the muscle tissue of the host," Simmons said.

Phillip nodded.

"The parasite eats the cells of the host to keep itself alive while reproducing exponentially," Simmons spoke with an utter fascination in his voice. "It specifically triggers the self-eating of the host's cells so it could feed on the rot."

"You mean it causes necrosis?" Phillip asked.

"Correct. While the PT-104 can survive off regular flesh, it primarily feeds on dead tissue. It also helps it reproduce faster."

Phillip pointed to the pig. "I'm seeing a lot of maggots. What is this?"

"That's PT-104 itself in its mature form," Simmons said. "The parasite starts off with a microscopic size, just like its eggs, but then it can grow to the size – and shape – of a maggot."

"Interesting. Any other abnormalities?"

"Yes," Simmons nodded fervently. "We thought the maggot eats the host until there is nothing else left to eat. Once the host dies, the parasite should naturally die shortly after."

"But that's not the case with PT-104?"

"No, it's not," Simmons exclaimed solemnly.

Phillip already knew the answer, so he didn't know why he insisted on asking. A part of him wanted to believe he was wrong, wanted to be proven wrong. Something told him that the parasite they were working with was way more than they bargained for.

Science could be deceiving, no matter what the experts said.

In a controlled environment, researchers could control a microorganism, expose it to certain variants and see how it reacted in the given situation. But that was all in a controlled environment. Out in the real world, those rules didn't apply.

Those tiny creatures were extremely smart, extremely adaptable. They could hold off mutating until the moment it served them. They could pretend to be dormant until a suitable victim was in their vicinity.

Phillip had worked with various microorganisms throughout his career, many of which were unknown to mankind. Some of them could withstand all kinds of things thrown at them. For some of them, even when the medication worked, they found a way to adapt and overcome its toxic effects.

Because of those extremely volatile cases, Phillip felt like they were in way over their heads with the PT-104.

"Okay, so tell me what happens," Phillip said.

"Let me show you." Simmons broke into a stride down the corridor.

WORK FROM HOME

I woke up multiple times in the early hours, my bedsheets covered in cold sweat. That was good, sweating was good, I thought. That was, at least, what my grandma always said whenever I had a fever. I kept falling in and out of consciousness until sunrise. I only got up because I needed to use the bathroom, and it was one of the most difficult things I had to do, because the moment I left the covers of the bed, icy cold enveloped me, causing my entire body to tremble like a car on a bumpy road.

I returned to bed after that and hermetically tucked myself in with blankets. Vaguely, I remember Catherine coming into my room at some point and saying that she had to go to work but that she would be home earlier and that I shouldn't hesitate to call her if I needed anything.

Between the drowsiness and the sickness, I don't think I had the strength to respond to her. In fact, I don't even know if she really came to my room if my fevered mind conjured up that scenario.

That day was a blur for me. I hardly ate anything, and when I did, it threatened to come right back out. Even drinking water took an effort. I texted Darren that I was sick, just to let him know why I wasn't as responsive as usually.

Even in my sick state, my mind conjured up scenarios where he would be beside me to take care of me while I was sick. Perhaps, I might have even dreamt about it at one point, but it's difficult to say.

I hardly remembered Catherine interacting with me when she came back home from work. She said something about me being a mess and urged me to eat soup and take some meds.

I spent another restless night trying to get a decent amount of sleep.

In the morning, I was still sick. In fact, I was sick for the next three or so days, and it didn't look like it was getting better at all. My wrist hurt like a bitch and I knew I had to go to the doctor's. For all I knew, I might have been suffering from a severe infection and this was my body's way of fighting it.

Catherine did most of the legwork for me. She called the doctor, drove me there, held me from collapsing while my head lolled left and right in the waiting room. The doctor ran some tests and whatnot – I honestly didn't remember everything he did – and then he said it was just a fever and dismissed me.

I was just relieved that it wasn't an infection. Catherine drove me back home and I slept for the rest of the day. Pretty soon, I got better. I was still fatigued from being bedridden, but I could finally do the majority of my daily activities, including work.

Since I wasn't sure how working from the office would affect me, I decided to work from home. Thank God for the flexibility my company offered. Yes, I would have more expenses for food those days, but I would be working from home.

One problem that I had with working from home is the fact that I easily got distracted. While I was at the office, I could write a line after line of code for hours without even noticing how much time had gone by, no problem. Even the murmurs of my co-workers didn't distract me, and if things got too loud, I could get earbuds and play music.

When I was home, however, my focus was pretty much non-existent. I coded a little bit, then switched tabs and my eyes accidentally fell on something interesting that stole my attention for a couple of minutes, then I looked away from the computer and thought about how the shelves needed reorganizing, or how the desk was dirty, and so on.

Despite the fact that working from home was only a temporary thing, and the fact that a lot of the employers were still skeptical about letting their employees work from home, who was to say that working from home wouldn't be a permanent expense-free solution for companies?

I had to be ready in case that happened someday, and that's why I made a system in which I would do "coding sprints," which was essentially an amount of time where I would have to focus on just coding without averting my gaze. As my focus got better, the amount of time would increase.

A lot of people didn't realize that focus is like a muscle – you need to train it. But it also depended on the environment. Anyway, aside from doing the sprints, I also made sure to remove anything that might distract me. That meant closing all unnecessary tabs, making sure not to be in the same room as the mess that beckoned me to clean it, no TV in the background, and similar.

"Well, someone's up early," Catherine said one morning when she woke up to get ready for work and saw me typing away on my laptop on the living room couch.

"Yeah. I want to get as much work done as possible so I can take it easier tomorrow, maybe call it a day around noon," I said.

"Lucky you. I got that stupid business trip to LA tomorrow," Catherine said, her voice croaky from just waking up.

"Oh, crap. I forgot all about that..." I said, dismayed.

She mentioned it a few weeks earlier, but with the date, the bite, the sickness, and everything else that transpired, it slipped my mind.

"How long did you say you're gonna be staying there?" I asked.

"A week. But since my vacation starts next Friday, I'll stay there a few extra days," Catherine said as she took out two pieces of sliced bread and slid them in the toaster.

"Oh. Wow," I tried to say as impassively as I could.

Truth be told, I wasn't looking forward to being all alone for the entire week. I'm an introvert, yes, and I got reminded of it every day whenever I spent too much time with people in meetings, but at the same time, I hated being alone for prolonged periods of time.

I first learned that when Catherine had a ten-day-long trip to Vegas. Although I spent most of my day in the office, returning to the empty apartment was still depressing. Then when I had to go to bed, paranoia started to creep in.

I got spooked easily, and even the slightest sound was enough to churn my brain into action of thinking what kind of a ghost, goblin, or a serial killer might be making the noise.

Are those pipes rattling? Or were they air ducts? What if we have a squatter living here and he sneaks out of his hole at night to watch me?

The fact that I've watched a few episodes of Unexplained Mysteries some days prior to Catherine's departure didn't help, either. And as things always went, when I went to bed, I imagined someone, or *something*, standing over me and watching me sleep. I kept swiveling to see if anyone stood there, expecting a lanky figure with long hair and ragged clothes to greet me with a creepy grin.

In the dark, furniture and other objects took on shapes that looked too humanoid, and I had to turn on the lights a few times just to make sure that wasn't the case. It was always the pile of clothes on the chair that looked like a monster, and when you turned on the lights, it was still just the heap of juxtaposed clothes.

If Darren were here, then I could invite him over for a movie or something and that would be perfectly okay. Like this, however, it would be a week of spending most of my days and nights alone. Actually, I could go to the office, but I honestly wanted to wait a little longer until I was feeling better.

"Hey, why don't you join me in LA in two weeks?" Catherine asked.

"Join you?" I raised my eyebrows.

"Yeah. We can have a mini vacation or something. You still have a lot of unused days, right?"

"Yeah. Hm."

The offer was enticing. It'd been a long time since I had a vacation, and an even longer time when I last visited LA. I bit my lip, thinking about the offer. Only a couple of things stopped me from actually agreeing right then and there. Number one, I wasn't sure if I was still going to be sick, and number two, I tried to remember if I had any important upcoming deadlines.

"I really wanna go," I said.

"But?" Catherine saw right through me.

"I need to wrap up some work here and all, and—
"

"Oh, come on. The company's not gonna stop just because you took a few days off," Catherine said.

The toaster pinged and the slices of bread jumped out, startling both Catherine and me. She sauntered back to it, pinched the bread between her fingers and tossed it on the plate while hissing and shaking her hand from being burned by the toast.

"You always burn yourself on the toast. You could, you know, wait for it to cool off," I said.

Catherine shook her head. "It's not the same when it cools off. If the toast isn't hot enough to cause blisters on the inside of your mouth, then it's not toast at all."

"Right."

"Okay, so…" she said as she took a bite of the toast. It crunched and crumbled onto the plate – and probably out of it, too. "Come with me to LA."

It came out as *hum wiv ee oo LA*.

I was already so close to agreeing, I just needed a reason to do it.

"Oh, what the hell, sure!" I threw my hands up.

"Yes!" Catherine squealed with excitement as she pumped her fist.

She ran over to me with the toast in her hand and wrapped her free hand around me. The savory smell of toast wafted my nostrils. My stomach growled in response, reminding me that it needed to be filled. Toast sounded great right about then.

"Okay," Catherine said. "I'll call you next week when I'm in LA so we can arrange where to meet up and all that."

"Okay, sounds good."

Catherine was right. I think I deserved a small vacation with all the hard work I put in. I got two promotions in less than three years and I think that was an admirable achievement. Yes, I needed to work hard for my next promotion, which was due in a year or so, but I also figured that my promotion wouldn't – and shouldn't! – be impacted by my choice to unwind a little and have a well-deserved vacation.

After Catherine left for work, I continued coding. A text from Darren reminded me that I might be gone for LA just in time when he returned, which meant we wouldn't see each other for a bit longer than expected. That was almost enough for me to cancel the trip, but I knew I couldn't put big plans like those on hold for someone who might or might not end up being my boyfriend.

My boyfriend. The tingling sensation in my stomach once again visited me. I wasn't sure if it was from still being sick or was it the butterflies of love doing their thing. I didn't care.

I had a lot of work to do if I wanted to stay ahead of the curve when I went on my vacation.

SYMPTOMS

As the day went on, I thought more and more about my upcoming trip to LA. When I first agreed to go, I did it on a whim. But now that I had more time to let it settle and think about it, I had a clearer view.

I don't like traveling. I know this is something you don't hear a lot, but there's nothing I hate more than trundling in a bus packed with sweaty people or being cooped up in an airplane seven miles above ground with a crying toddler. I love visiting new places, I love sightseeing, I love trying out new food and all that, but just the multiple-hour-long trip there and back is enough to dissuade me from going.

Still, I looked forward to going to LA. I guess it's because I haven't done anything new in a while. My destinations have been home-work with the occasional stop elsewhere. It's unhealthy.

I even neglected my hobby of learning French. I know learning a language is supposed to be a serious commitment and not a hobby, but the reason why I viewed it as such was because the moment it turns into an obligation is the moment I'll stop doing it.

My books had been collecting dust on the shelves as well. I had a ton that I binge-bought before my promotion, back when I still had the time to read, but never actually read.

I keep telling myself that I'll continue working like this just a little longer. Just until the next promotion and then I can take it easy. But it's never like that, is it?

As soon as you land a promotion, you have to work more, which leaves you with even less time than before.

Either that, or the promotion never comes and we're stuck perpetually working our asses off, waiting for the day to finally be able to take it easy. There's also a bit of workaholism there, too.

If you've ever worked weekends and then stopped, you'll know that you suddenly feel unproductive on those days off. Your fingers are itching, you're restless, and you feel like you just have to do something, anything, just to get some work done.

The following day, Catherine left for her trip. We had a heartfelt goodbye and I had to fight not to get emotional. It's stupid, but goodbyes always got me emotional. The moment she left, the apartment felt vacuous.

I turned on the TV just to have some voices accompanying me. I spent the night watching TV shows – 70 percent of the time deciding what to watch, the rest of the time actually watching – and eating popcorn. I fell asleep on the couch at one point.

What awoke me was a vivid nightmare.

In my dream, I was on a trail in the middle of a foggy forest – or a park, it was impossible to tell. It was so foggy that I could hardly see a few feet in front of me. I thought I saw shadows slinking left and right just out of my view, merging with the thick mist surrounding me.

I heard growling from somewhere, but it was impossible to tell where it was coming from. Wherever I turned, the growling seemed to slip away, just enough to render me unable to pinpoint its location.

A wrinkled snout baring its sharp teeth came into view. The beast, which I instantly assumed was a mangy dog, snarled so violently at me that its skin pulled back from its mouth, revealing rotted, black gums.

Drool dribbled from its lower jaw, dripping on the floor in anticipation of the meal it was about to have. I backpedaled, but then a similar growling came behind me. As I pivoted, I saw more snouts, dozens… no hundreds of them, all pointed at me, all snarling and baring their teeth, ready to tear me to pieces.

Just as the first one lunged at me, its jaw unhinged, ready to sink its teeth into my flesh, and I woke up with a start.

I could still vividly hear the snarling in my head. It was so intense that my head automatically spun left and right to scan the room for any wild beasts. Nothing but silence. The lights were still on, the TV off. It must have automatically turned off after a while.

My hand reached toward my wrist to scratch an incessant itch, and then pulled back as I winced in pain. I got into a ramrod sitting position and looked at my wrist.

"Shit," I said as I stood up.

The scab glistened with something dark and I knew then that I had accidentally reopened it with scratching. Accompanied with the realization of what I had done, the pain manifested. It was a low, pulsating sensation. I rushed into the bathroom and put my wrist under the water.

That caused the pain to intensify. Blood and pieces of crusted scabs and skin washed off into the sink, leaving a bloodied wound. I closed the tap and dabbed the injury with a towel. Even touching it gently was agonizing. The pulsating had turned into a burning sensation which slowly morphed into tingling.

I removed the towel from the wrist and looked at it. While most of the bite mark was still covered in scabs, the part that I had accidentally scratched was bloodied. Thick red coated the top of the open wound. I looked at the towel. Traces of various shades of red, something even going to very dark, stained it.

Slowly, I put my fingers around the open wound and squeezed. The pain made me wince, but I muscled through it. Thick blood oozed out of the wound, like ketchup out of a tube. It was laced with hues of something orange and… black?

I cringed at the sight of it.

The wound should have been healed by all accounts, but instead, it looked like the thin brown scab was the only thing holding the blood from spilling out. I washed off the excess blood and spread the skin around the bite mark.

It was deep. I only had a second to peek before more blood congealed out of the wound. I washed that off, too. The blood fell out of my wrist in chunks. In fact, when I looked at the sink, I saw small pieces of coagulated blood strewn all around, refusing to wash off under the water.

I felt bile climbing into my throat at the thought of how much it reminded me of raspberry jam. Was my entire injury like that? I had to know. I wiped my wrist dry. More blood piled out of my wound, but I ignored it.

With my thumb and forefinger, I pinched the scab that jutted out on one end. Slowly and meticulously, I pulled at it. It taped off my skin, like a zipper on a jacket. A bloody line formed in its trail, painful to watch and painful to feel.

I thought that pulling the scab would reveal a thin line of rose scar tissue where the skin would grow out later, but instead, there was blood. An abundance of it. The scabs were essentially a dam to hold the blood in, but the interior of my wound hadn't healed one bit.

Just like the one I accidentally scratched, thick red surfaced on my newly opened wound. I wished that I could return the thin streak of scab back to how it was so the wound was closed, but I had pulled way too far already.

The scab in my hand was like a thin string of cheese. It felt morbidly satisfying to pull, as grotesque as it was. I yanked off the rest of it and then dropped the thin, curled piece of dead skin into the sink. It looked like a dead worm among all the chunks of coagulated blood.

Now, my entire wrist was covered in red. I ran the water and swiped the blood off with the palm of my hand. The sensation sent daggers through my arm, which caused my fingers to convulse, as if zapped with an electric shock.

I washed off the excess blood, leaving a clean open wound, but that lasted for barely a second before more blood climbed to the top. The more I washed, the more blood seemed to appear. The sink was covered in watered-down red that rapidly ran down the drain, with more and more waves covering it.

Despite the immense pain, I kept scrubbing the blood off. I was determined not to have a single droplet of blood coming out of the wound. Chunks of blood fell into the sink with wet splatters, covering the entire thing like a field of dropped strawberries reduced to mush.

Watery pus came out as well, mixed in with the blood, but I ignored it.

I stopped when my eyes caught a glimpse of something black coming out of my wound. I brought my wrist closer to my face to observe what it was. Perhaps a blood vessel that I accidentally scrubbed out?

Something foul permeated my nostrils. I couldn't pinpoint what it was, but it smelled rotten. Disgusting as it was, I squeezed my wrist again to get the black stuff out. It came out with a squelching sound, like toothpaste coming out of a tube that was nearing its end.

Something yellow appeared in the black stuff. I squeezed harder and harder, determined to get it out. It was impossible to tell what the mush was. The squeezed-out paste plopped into the sink and I stared at it. It was red, black, and a tiny bit of something yellow in it.

I turned the tap water off. The water running was too loud and I needed silence to focus. I brought my head closer to the tiny curl of black and squinted at it. I jabbed it with one finger to roll it over, determined to find out what it was.

It stubbornly clung to the ceramic of the sink, so I pushed it harder. A part of it broke off. I gazed at the tiny yellow thing and recoiled with a loud gasp.

My hands shot toward my mouth to clasp them over my mouth, but stopped short when I figured that my hands were tainted. I looked down at my wrist. The blood had stopped coming out. My hands were shaking so badly that I thought I was having a seizure.

I couldn't inhale properly. My throat had constricted and breathing in felt like trying to get a whiff of air through a blocked straw. I vaguely became aware of the fact that I was whimpering as well as hyperventilating.

I had to take another look at what was in the sink. What I saw couldn't possibly be right, could it? No, I must have imagined it.

Tentatively, I took a step forward, my knees threatening to buckle under my weight. I desperately needed to hold onto something, but touching anything felt so wrong in that moment. I jackknifed at the waist, leaning closer to the sink, now shaking entirely from head to toe. I suppressed the urge to pull my hair back. I didn't want to touch anything with my hands.

I stared at the black piece of whatever it was that fell out of my wound. Specifically, I focused on the tiny yellow rice-like grain. I blinked.

The yellow thing wiggled.

FESTER

I hadn't seen it wrong after all. It really did move. I blinked furiously at the sink, trying to convince myself it was just my overactive imagination and sleep deprivation playing tricks on me.

As if the maggot in the lesion understood me, it wriggled more furiously, its tiny head swaying left and right, as if waving to me.

Hey, I'm right here! Yes, I'm real, don't look so shocked!

I got even closer because there's no way this thing that came out of the inside of my body could possibly be real, no way in hell. Still, I retained some distance. I was afraid that coming too close could cause it to shoot out of its black prison and get in my eye.

For a moment, I imagined the maggot squirming under my eyelid while I futilely tried to get it out. It would crawl behind my eye where I couldn't reach it and lay eggs there. Days later, more worms would plop out of my eyelids.

I felt the skin on my entire body crawling at that.

For a while longer, I stared at the yellow maggot in the black chunk that fell out of my flesh. As if my eyes only just then adjusted to the sight, I saw another yellow grain. And then another, and another, until a dozen or so adorned the chunk of flesh.

All of them wiggled disgustingly, each in their own direction, as if trying to break free of the tomb that held them in place. And one of them managed to do so. It plopped into the sink next to the black mass, where it continued slithering in a random direction.

I ran the water at full pressure. The jet didn't even reach them, so I tore off a bunch of toilet paper and collected the maggots and the black thing into it. I held my breath as I scooped them up and tossed them in the toilet. Never before has flushing felt so relieving.

Watching the bundled-up toilet paper flush in the swirl of water made me catch my breath a little bit. But then I remembered the sink that was still riddled with raspberry jam and my open wound and–

I instinctively looked down at my wound. If there was one maggot, there was probably a ton of them. More blood had surfaced on my wound, but I couldn't see anything yellow swimming in it. Just the thought of having more of those things inside me caused the sickness in my stomach to exacerbate.

I could no longer hold my dinner down.

I bent down and shot a projectile of vomit into the toilet. It was mostly in liquid form. I spat multiple times and flushed before wading back to the sink. I honestly just wanted to pass out in that moment and not wake up until this was all over.

I rinsed the sink, scraping off every last bit of the stuff that came out of me until it was white and glistening once more. I then washed my hands so vigorously that the skin on my fingers was red. I washed my wrists and my forearms, scrubbing hard, ignoring the pain in my wound.

The entire time, I gawped at the open bite mark, expecting more maggots to plop out of it. In that moment, I wanted to dig through the wound until I reached the bone just so I could make sure the little creatures weren't buried deep inside my arm.

I imagined them squirming inside me, feasting on my flesh, mating, and laying eggs, letting their offspring hatch and create more and more of them so they could eat me from the inside out.

The vivid thought of that made me want to chop off my own hand. Back when I was a kid, my cousin Susan came to sleep over while her mom was on a business trip. One night, my mom noticed that Susan had been scratching her head a lot in her sleep. She snuck up to Susan and checked her head for lice. Sure enough, she found some.

I spent the next few days avoiding Susan like the plague, dreading the thought of having those little bugs living in my hair and sucking on my blood. The crawling sensation was so intense that I was seriously tempted to shave my entire head just to get rid of them.

My mom had checked my hair and confirmed that I was lice-free, much to my relief. The fear of having anything parasitic living inside me, whether it's tapeworms, head lice, or anything else, overshadowed all my other fears when I was a kid.

I had completely forgotten about it until the night I saw the maggots emerging from my wound. Once my wound was completely clean and no more coagulated blood came out, I took some hydrogen peroxide from the medicine cabinet and poured a handful on my wrist.

It burned like crazy, but I didn't care. I just wanted it clean. The hydrogen formed bubbles and foam, which I understood meant a sure infection, right? I kept rinsing and pouring more and more until the foam stopped appearing.

I then put a gauze on my wrist and wrapped it so tightly that the circulation of blood in my hand stopped. I loosened it a little, but only a little. My reasoning for tightening it so hard was to stop the stupid maggots from crawling out while I slept. I had to keep the wound sealed until I got to a doctor.

But then a terrifying thought came to my mind.

What if the maggots start panicking because they have no way out, so they start eating through my flesh for a way out, kind of like the rats in a heated bucket torture method?

No, stop thinking about that, Melanie. Stop it. Call your doctor. Now.

That's exactly what I did. I dialed the doctor's number with trembling hands. It took me a moment to actually tap on the option to call him. The tips of my fingers hurt like hell, but that was good. It made me feel better because the pain meant I had thoroughly cleaned my hands.

I hadn't even bothered looking at what time it was when I called Doctor Mills. I impatiently waited while the phone rang, the pause between each ring seemingly lasting for an eternity. I was about to hang up when I heard the distinct click that meant someone answered.

"Hello?" a gruff, groggy voice asked.

It was audible that he'd been sleeping. I was too worried about the maggots to care whether he would tell me off for calling him at this hour.

"Doctor Mills?" I asked. "It's Melanie."

It took everything within me not to let my tongue unroll and just dump all the information on him that I thought was relevant. I needed to make sure he was listening first.

"Melanie?" he asked, his words slurred and his tone droopy. "What's going on? What time is it?"

"I'm so sorry for calling you this late, Doctor, but I... I think there's something wrong with me. There... there are m-maggots in my wound."

That last sentence barely came out. I vaguely became aware of the fact that I was crying. The accumulated stress and panic must have finally broken me.

"Calm down, Melanie. Tell me what happened," Doctor Mills said after a long pause.

I sniffled, shuddered, and once I regained my composure, I told him what happened to me as calmly and slowly as I could. My tongue threatened to speed up and convey information with more urgency. It felt as though every minute that passed was a minute more maggots would hatch inside me.

I had been talking so fast that it took me a moment to realize Doctor Mills was interrupting me to say something. I stopped and clung on to every word he said. He was my salvation. He would fix me. Just hearing his voice made me feel all the better.

"Okay, Melanie. Can you come to my office now?" he asked.

"Yes!" I exclaimed, nodding fervently, even though he couldn't see my face.

"Do you have anyone to take you there?"

"N-no. My roommate is on a t-trip. But I can come, it's fine," I said through gasps and tears.

"Okay. Just calm down. Everything will be all right. Okay? If you can't come to the office, please call me and I'll come by your house."

"Th-thank you, Doctor Mills," I said. "I-I'm on m-my way now."

"Okay. I'll see you in a bit."

As soon as I hung up, I cried like a little baby. It was tears of relief mixed with panic and worry. God, why wasn't Catherine here? Of all the days, this is when I needed her the most. She would know what to say to make me feel better. She would assure me everything would be okay.

But she wasn't here and I had to deal with this alone. I got dressed, grabbed my wallet and car keys, and flew out of the apartment.

DOCTOR

"No signs of necrosis or infection," Doctor Howard Mills said.

The words sounded like the judge in a courtroom striking his desk with a gavel, proclaiming that all charges are dropped. I could physically imagine holding a heavy, toddler-sized rock in my hands and dropping it by my feet the moment Doctor Mills spoke up.

As much as I desperately wanted – no, *needed* – to believe that conclusion, a part of me remained tentative and skeptical. What if the doctor was wrong?

"But… what about the…" I started, but my throat closed up.

"The maggots?" he asked.

He made a face that I couldn't recognize. It could have been him trying to suppress laughter while giving me a reassuring stare. It also could have been the fact that I woke him up at 2 A.M. in the morning and raised an alarm big enough for him to think I was dying and come down to his office.

"What you described to me sounds like wound myiasis, which is not what I'm seeing here," Doctor Mills said.

I almost thought I could detect accusation in his tone. *Nope, nothing is wrong with you, Melanie. You made me drive out here for nothing. That's fine, I start work at seven in the morning, might as well stay up now.*

"But I saw them *moving*," I exclaimed, emphasizing the final word.

"What you saw couldn't have been maggots, Melanie," the doctor said as he sat across from me.

For a moment, the shadows on his face made him look ten years older.

"So then, what was it?" I asked.

I was still shaking from the whole ordeal. I could no longer tell if Doctor Mills' office was cold or if I was still under stress.

The doctor inhaled deeply through his nose and pensively looked at the ceiling before replying, "It could have been scabs. It could have been blood that looked like it. You said you noticed it as soon as you woke up, correct?"

I understood what he was implying here. I had woken up and was too tired, which caused my groggy mind to see things that weren't really there. As much as I wanted to go into hysterics and tell the doctor that it wasn't the case, I also wanted to remain calm and reasonable.

For all I knew, he could be right. A thought occurred to me that I should have brought the maggots – or whatever they were – in the paper towel for him to see. No, that would never work, no way.

Having those little bastards squirm and slither in every direction in my car while I drove, only to find them later on crawling over my seat and pants would probably be enough for me to drive the car into the closest body of water.

"Look, I understand you're worried, Melanie," Doctor Mills said, breaking my train of thought. "But I can assure you, you're perfectly fine. Yes, your wound is not healed, but that's all right. Just give it time. Keep it bandaged and don't touch it for a few weeks."

I bit my lip. I wasn't 100 percent convinced, but no other questions popped into my mind about what the doctor might have potentially missed. Besides, he was the doctor, not me.

"I'm really sorry for dragging you out of bed so late, Doctor Mills," I uttered.

The doctor flashed me a PR grin and stood up.

"If you have any questions or concerns, feel free to call me, Melanie. And try not to worry too much. You're perfectly healthy, okay?"

I left the doctor's office feeling much better. I felt like I needed some food from the stress that I had suffered, so I stopped at a burger place. There was something special about eating food in the middle of the night; something sinful about it that made it so much more appetizing.

It wasn't illegal, but it sure felt like it sometimes. I guess it reminds me of the times when I lived with my parents. When I was a kid, I had a phase when I would wake up certain nights with a crazy hankering for food.

I would sneak into the kitchen and rummage through the fridge and the cupboards looking for loot. I especially loved eating things in crinkly bags. I guess it was the fact that they made such loud noise and threatened to wake up my parents, which made me want to have what was inside even more.

After satisfying my desire for food, I would always tiptoe back to bed, satisfied for managing to pull off the crime in such a sneaky way. That is until morning, when my mom would ask me what I was doing in the kitchen last night.

The fact that I'd been caught and suffered no consequences somehow killed the magic of the plundering. It eliminated the sense of accomplishment that I had of getting the forbidden goods without getting caught. Still, I continued sneaking at nights to the fridge while being cautious not to make too much noise, just for my own sake.

That habit followed me to my college life until I realized that I was an adult and no longer needed to worry about it. If I wanted to eat cake at 3 AM. then I could do so.

Anyway, after wolfing down the burger, I drove home and collapsed into bed from exhaustion.

PARK

I slept much longer than I planned to. I could usually tell upon waking up if it was late or not. I don't know how exactly I have that superpower, but I just do. Maybe I kind of determine how well-rested I am and estimate based on that what time it is.

Anyway, the sun was high up in the sky and the birds chattered loud outside my window when I opened my eyes. I had a headache, but dismissed it as a result of a bad sleeping position.

The first thing I did was take a look at my bandaged arm. The image of maggots crawling under the white fabric occupied my mind's eye, but I quickly dismissed it. It's amazing how one reassuring word from a doctor can make us calm down.

I didn't have to work today, and I desperately wanted to get out of the apartment for some fresh air. The problem was, I couldn't go jogging or working out yet because I still felt remnants of fatigue from my fever lingering, plus I didn't want to get my wound sweaty.

Still, taking a walk in the park wouldn't be nearly as strenuous and it would give me some much-needed respite. As much as I preferred staying inside and watching shows, reading, or playing video games, I had a limit as to how long I could stay cooped up under a roof.

I'm not sure if it's cabin fever or anything like that, but if I stay inside for too long without seeing the sun, I start to feel like I'm losing my mind. I once knew a guy who was a total hermit like that.

His name was Ulysses and he worked an online teaching job from home. He never left his apartment. And I mean never. He spent the entire day cooped up in front of his computer, only opening the door when his food delivery arrived.

I met Ulysses when Catherine and I visited Portland. Ulysses had hosted a big dinner party at his apartment and invited a group of people, Catherine included. I didn't know the guy, but Catherine did, and she assured me it would be totally okay for me to go with her.

Before we entered, Catherine gave me a fair warning that Ulysses is a little... weird. Weird was one way of putting it.

Ulysses was a tall, overweight guy with disheveled hair, and a round head into which bovine eyes were affixed. When we first entered, he greeted us with a bear hug that knocked the air out of me.

When Catherine said there would be ten people at the party, I expected an apartment spacious enough to perform gymnastics in the living room. Instead, the one-bedroom studio apartment had us all crammed like sardines and elbowing each other.

Plates and silverware dropped, cups of drinks spilled, but despite all of that, the people were in relatively high spirits. I say relatively because the atmosphere was great while people talked to each other, but the moment Ulysses spoke up, his booming, opera-singer-like voice caused all heads to snap in his direction.

I hated thinking this way, but he totally reminded me of one of those stereotypical bullies in the movies from the nineties. But Ulysses was no bully despite the looks.

Things got even weirder as the night rolled on.

Ulysses brought out a fleshlight that he showed to the guests. Dead silence draped the air when he spoke *about it with exuberance that no human should display when talking about a fleshlight to a group of strangers.*

"It's really good. You wanna try it?" he asked as he nudged it to one of the guys who grimaced and said something along the lines of, I'm not sticking my dick in your girlfriend, much to the roaring laughter of the group.

"What are you all laughing at?!" Ulysses exploded and once again silence descended on the room.

Ulysses must have realized the awkwardness because he forced a nervous chuckle a moment later and said he was only joking.

I'm only telling you all of this so that you would get a glimpse into how uncomfortable interactions with Ulysses were. I wish that was the end of it, but the dinner wouldn't even begin to describe the incidents with Ulysses.

Anyway, after dinner was done and we were sufficiently away from the building where Ulysses' eyes couldn't possibly reach us from the apartment window, I asked Catherine what in the holy hell is wrong with her to hang out with a guy like him.

She muttered something about him being a nice guy despite his flaws. I gave her a look and she agreed that it would be the last time we met up with Ulysses. From everything I was able to figure, he wasn't a bad person, just socially awkward. In fact, he was a gracious host, maybe even a little too much with his stampeding from guest to guest and getting in their faces to ask if the food was okay.

Unlike the courteous manner in which the waiters at restaurants ask it, Ulysses' question sounded more like a threat. "Is the food good? It better be, or I'll snap your goddamn neck."

The moment I stepped out and felt the cool breeze enveloping my neck and face, I felt renewed. Things like those filled me with exuberance beyond verbal explanation. I went to the closest park, staving off my desire to break into a relentless jog.

Not a lot of people were at the park yet. Close to afternoon, parents would bring their kids, and pet owners would walk their dogs, filling the park with jovial voices and positive energy. I preferred the silence and was determined to take it in as much as I possibly could.

I put in my earbuds and listened to some serene music while strolling down the trail under the evergreens. The noon sun peered between the branches, sending warm rays of sunlight on my face whenever I stepped out from the shade.

As I looked to the left, my eyes fell on something that made me freeze. I could no longer hear the lyrics of the song, even though I'd been singing along with them in my head up until that point.

A stray dog walked between the trees slinking in an out of view. He was about fifty feet away, unaware of me, occasionally sniffing the ground before moving onto the next spot. My heart hammered against my chest.

I pulled out my earbuds. The song I'd been listening to turned into a muffled whisper. It hadn't even occurred to me that I might run into a stray dog while walking in the park, but now that I'd seen one, I was petrified.

Instantly, I was brought back to the night with Darren when the dog bit me in the park. My wrist burned and pulsated, as if the bite was fresh and not weeks old. The dog turned its head toward me and wagged its tail.

Don't come here, don't come here, don't come here, I chanted in my mind, too terrified to move.

The dog turned away and left. I breathed a tentative sigh of relief and went in the opposite direction of the dog, keeping an eye out for him. My legs felt weak. A shiver penetrated through my thick clothes and prickled my skin ever so gently.

I'd suddenly had enough of the park. It was time to go home. The casual stroll up until then transformed into a hurried gait as my mind raced to figure out where the closest exit was.

The entire park suddenly felt dangerous. Every rustle of the leaves, every bark in the distance, every silhouette among the trees seemed like they were out to get me. Why were there so many stray animals in Seattle? Animal Control really needed to do something about it.

You can sue the city, Catherine's voice reverberated in my skull.

Let me tell you, had I gotten bitten again that day, I sure as hell would have sued the shit out of them. Physical damage, emotional damage, all kinds of damages. It wasn't even about the money, I didn't care about that. It was about teaching them a lesson so they could take such a public issue seriously.

Nothing got the government to act faster than slapping their pockets.

As soon as I was out of the park, relief flooded me. I looked over my shoulder a couple of times to make sure no animals were following me and then hurried back toward the apartment. My heart had stopped jackhammering by then and the stability in my legs was back.

With the fear gone, I replayed the scene in the park. Did I really just get scared of a dog? The animal I thought was so sacred and beautiful, all because one of them bit me?

I felt horrible for thinking that way. In my mind, I saw myself as Aunt Shelly's newest husband, Artie – the fifth husband in her lifetime. Artie was an avid animal hater and very openly showed it.

He talked about his disgust for people who love animals more than children, how dogs shouldn't be allowed inside, how they are a waste of time, space, and money, and similar ugly comments. The most ironic thing? Aunt Shelly's daughter had a pug that she always brought to her visits and allowed it to sit at the table just to spite Artie.

That always brought a smile to my face.

And that's why I felt so ashamed of myself when I left the park. I convinced myself that the fear I felt was rational. It was a stray animal after all, and I'd already been bitten once. I was not like Artie and would never allow myself to become like him.

I felt pretty exhausted by the time I reached home. The walk, coupled with the cold, must have knocked me out. I heated up some leftover macaroni and cheese and slumped onto the couch after eating.

It had been a while since I've read anything, so I grabbed a sci-fi book from the shelves. I had been wanting to either watch a sci-fi movie or read a sci-fi book for a while now, so I hoped the one in my hand wouldn't disappoint.

As soon as I opened the first page, my eyes became heavy. I could hardly focus on the black-on-white letters in front of me. I read the words, but none of them bore any meaning.

Every time I blinked, my eyes stayed closed for longer and longer. I squeezed them shut and opened. My eyes burned, as if I had just spent too much time in front of the TV.

I slammed the book shut and tossed it on the coffee table. Reading would be impossible right now. Determined to take a nap, I got into a more comfortable position. I didn't even bother setting my alarm. If I ended up napping for four hours, then so be it. I didn't give a damn.

A muffled buzzing that came from somewhere outside was soothing. I don't remember when I fell asleep, but I do remember waking up to immense pain in my wrist.

ROT

It wasn't just a nagging irritation. It was full-blown pain. I remember feeling it even in my dream, like when you're asleep and you need to pee, and you relieve yourself in the dream, but your bladder continues screaming.

My wrist felt as if someone was digging knives into my bite mark. I winced and hissed as I gently put my palm over the bandaged wrist. Even through the fabric, it felt hot as the devil's crotch. I went into the bathroom and unwrapped the bandage.

Layer after layer came off until only the gauze remained. I knew unsticking it would probably be painful if it clung to the crusted blood. I suppressed the urge to rip it off as I would a plaster and slowly peeled it off.

A sticky sound came from my wrist as the gauze unrolled, revealing dried blood and–

At first, my brain couldn't process what I was seeing. A patch of black coated my arm with a sea of yellow grains that squirmed on top of it, climbing over each other and burrowing under each other. A bunch of the grains stubbornly clung to the gauze, while some dropped below on the floor and into the sink.

Then the smell hit me.

A disgusting, rotting smell that came from my wound and invaded my nostrils, instantly causing the undigested macaroni and cheese to swirl inside my stomach, threatening to get out.

I wanted to scream at the party of maggots feasting on my arm, but I couldn't. I had no voice. And then, as if a switch in my brain had been flicked, I understood what I was looking at.

I screamed at the top of my lungs. When I was out of breath, I screamed again, over and over, until my throat became raspy and sore. I turned on the tap water and put my wrist under it, swatting violently at it, trying to get the maggots off, but too disgusted to touch them.

They washed out of my wound and fell into the sink, a bevy of them washing down the drain while their lucky brothers and sisters remained in the sink, wiggling their heads feebly. Despite having no eyes, I swear I could feel their microscopic gazes on me.

More and more washed off until the sink was full of tiny grains. When the majority was washed away, my gaze fell on the wound.

It was no longer a bite mark. It was an entire crater, deep, black with rot, yellow with pus, crimson with remnants of blood and muscle. A meager number of maggots remained in there, clinging to my flesh like flies to food. I swatted at them, but only a few budged.

I incessantly slapped the remaining three, but they were still there. Upon looking closer, I noticed they were burying themselves into my flesh. If they got inside, I would be totally and utterly fucked.

Using my other hand, I pinched the first one between my thumb and forefinger. It was tiny and I could barely feel it. It was wet, gooey, and slippery. It squirmed more violently against my touch, tickling my flesh.

I pulled but my fingers slipped. I tried again, and they slipped once more. I tried a third time, and this time, I managed to get a good enough grasp. I squeezed, feeling the maggot's elastic body squishing under my touch.

Ever so slowly, I pulled. It was slightly longer than I thought it would be. More than half of it had been buried in my tissue. Once it was out, it gyrated left and right in my grip, as if complaining that I had pried it away from its new home.

This one was bigger than the rest. Its translucent, milky body visibly showed off its disgusting insides that dimpled under my squeeze. Its black proboscis snipped and opened intermittently, as if threatening to bite whatever came near it.

I put it under the stream of water and let it wash down the drain.

Two more remained.

I grabbed the next one and pulled it out with ease. I pinched the third one as well, but before I could yank it out, it snapped in half. *Shit.* I looked down at the half of the maggot in my flesh and watched as it wriggled deeper and deeper into the cavity it had dug.

"No!" I proclaimed through my teeth, tossing the other half under the water and reaching for the maggot.

Just as I grabbed it, it slipped. I pressed my fingers against the exposed wound and dug deeper. The maggot was one step ahead. Before I could grab it, it was gone, absorbed in the mass of red.

I hyperventilated. It was inside me. It would lay more eggs there.

I opened the medicine cabinet and rummaged through it, knocking half of the items into the sink and on the floor. I found a pair of tweezers. Exactly what I was looking for.

That maggot wasn't going to get away from me. I brought the tweezers closer to the wound and then sunk them in. The pain was out of this world, but my conviction to find the final maggot was stronger.

The tweezers were embedded deep in my flesh, sending scalding pain through my arm. I resisted the urge to contract my fingers as much as I could. Somehow, that made me think that the muscles in my forearm would clench as well, making it harder to locate the body invader.

It was impossible to tell what I was grabbing with the tweezers. Everything was wet and mushy. I pinched, then pulled out. Nothing but blood. I did it again, and again, and again, until I felt something squishy coming between the heads. I pulled, slowly, gently, while gripping the maggot with enough force to not let it escape.

What came out was impossible to identify. It was black, coated in red, and–

I thought I saw squirming on the tweezers. I immediately put the tips under the running tap and watched in relish as the maggot washed down the drain.

There. All gone.

I looked down and noticed more grains on my other hand. Then on my shirt. Then at my feet, crawling up my socks. I slithered out of my clothes until I was fully naked and tossed them all in the washing machine. I slammed the lid shut and frantically pressed the buttons until it roared to life. I had no idea if maggots could drown, but I sure as hell hoped they could.

If not, I would fucking burn the clothes down.

My entire body was itchy. My hands consistently swatted at my skin, expecting something small and squishy, alive to the touch and wriggly to come in contact. I had to sterilize everything. The bathroom, the living room, me. It all had to be cleaned thoroughly.

The first thing I did was prepare all the disinfectants in the apartment, all the paper towels, all the mops, everything that I could use for cleaning. I started with the bathroom. I had no intention of stopping until the place was as sterile as a pharmacy.

I scrubbed the floor with such intensity that my muscles hurt. My wound pulsated and burned. Only then did the pain come back, and even then, I was too focused on cleaning to pay attention to it.

My eyes occasionally fell on my wrist, mostly because I wanted to make sure no other maggots were going to crawl out of there. The hues of jaundice that coated my rotting wound gave me pause, but upon looking better, I noticed it was only pus.

Thank goodness.

I didn't stop until the entire house was clean from top to bottom. By then, hours had passed. My entire body ached, especially my back, but I paid it no mind.

The tickling and itching sensation was the only thing that bothered me. I continuously felt something brushing against the nape of my neck, the unreachable part of my back, even the insides of my ears. I scratched myself so hard that my skin turned red – I hadn't realized this until I looked at myself in the mirror later.

Once everything was clean and all the maggots disposed of, I stepped into the shower and ran hot water. It burned, but it felt good. I didn't want the maggots on, and in, my body to be comfortable. I wanted them to burn and wash off.

I stared down at my feet as the water from the showerhead ran down my head and body. Tiny rice-like grains plopped on the ceramic bathtub with wet splotches. I must have spent a solid thirty minutes or so under the scalding water. The steam was so thick that I could hardly see anything in the bathroom. The temperature of it also made me feel woozy.

As much as I hated the thought of it, it was time to get out.

I made sure to double-check my entire body before doing so, rinsing my hair, glancing at my wound again – it was puffy and swollen and the water made it smell even worse – and scrutinizing my toes to see if any of them had wedged in between.

I also checked the floor outside the shower. Everything tiny looked like a maggot in that moment. Anything grainy looked like a bug. I even looked at the ceiling, fully expecting some of those little fuckers to cling to the wall and fall into my eyes as soon as I was under them.

The crawling sensation on my skin had lessened after taking a shower, but I still had the urge to scratch myself. I wiped the foggy mirror and stared at my reflection. Jesus, I didn't look like myself one bit.

My eyes were bloodshot. My skin was pale, almost verging on gray. My lips were dry and cracked. Blood decorated the corner of my mouth. I wiped, but it refused to come off. It was painful.

I leaned toward the mirror and examined what it was. It looked like a cold sore, only a little more severe – an uneven red patch, blistery, with red and yellow in the center where it was chipped. I touched it with the tip of my finger and recoiled at the pain it produced.

My eyes fell on the knuckles of my fingers. They were badly abraded, to the point of skin giving way to the flesh. I must have scrubbed the floors and other surfaces too hard.

The upper part of my chest looked no better than my face. Millions of red specks adorned my skin from the collarbone all the way down to the top of my breasts. Some of them were open, but most looked like blisters – swollen, red, looking like one tiny puncture with a needle would cause them to explode.

The lack of pain surprised me.

My thighs were in a similar condition. I pressed down on one of the blisters on my chest. It didn't hurt unless I squeezed too hard. I wanted to pop them badly, but I figured it would be best to leave them alone. I wouldn't want another open would prone to infections.

I was exhausted by then. My feet were killing me and I felt like I would collapse if I continued standing just a few minutes longer. I desperately needed to sleep. My eyelids kept closing on their own. My entire body throbbed with pain.

No, not before I'm done checking myself out. I brushed my hair, stroke my stroke all the way from the root, to get any lingering maggots out, in case there were any. The brush got stuck on one of the tufts.

I tried unsticking it, but it wouldn't budge. I yanked the brush and the tuft of my hair came off my scalp with a tearing sound. I looked at the roots of the hair follicles. Bloodied, with dead skin on them, but no maggots. I tossed the hair into the sink, too tired to flush it down the toilet.

I was so tired.

My wrist, my chest, my legs, my fingers, and now my scalp all burned with a steady, annoying pain. I dropped the hairbrush into the sink and strode out of the bathroom. I carefully eyed the floor for any maggots waiting to ambush me.

No. I was thorough. None remained after I was done cleaning. Not only did I disinfect all the surfaces of the apartment, but I used a steam mop for a second round to make sure anything residual met its demise.

I got into bed and folded my arm in a way that I could look at the wrist where the rotting crater was. If anything came crawling out of my wounds, I would be here to apprehend it.

Since it was still bleeding slightly, I kept a towel next to me to dab the wound whenever too much blood seeped out.

I desperately tried to keep my eyes open. I needed to keep my guard up.
Sleep overtook me before long.

CATHERINE

"He just never stops talking," Yasmin said when they finally exited the meeting room.

Catherine felt the same way. The meetings seemed to last for a small eternity whenever James Lillard hosted them. First there was the technology check and making sure everything worked properly, then there was the mandatory small talk because Lillard didn't believe in starting a meeting without first asking everyone how their weekend or trip was.

Worst of all, however, must have been the fact that James Lillard was the only one participating in the meeting. For over an hour, his high-pitched voice was the only thing that filled the room while the rest of the attendees yawned, stared into their laps, and struggled to keep their eyes open.

"Yeah, he's really annoying," Catherine responded. "I know we shouldn't say that and that it's company culture, yadda-yadda, but he is just so frigging boring! We might as well be listening to someone read the contents on the back of a food product."

"And I don't know why he wants us all in a one-hour-long meeting when he could have easily just sent us the minutes!" Yasmin agreed.

The two women strode down the company corridors, gossiping about James Lillard with buoyant voices. It was okay to do so here in LA because it wasn't Catherine's office. Back in Seattle, if someone heard her, she might end up with a seat in front of HR.

It happened to one of her co-workers. He said in passing once how the collaborating teams did almost none of the work and took credit for it. Not one day later, he was sent to sensitivity training. Absolute bullshit in Catherine's mind, not being able to talk about what they wanted.

"You think he makes these kinds of preparations and speeches whenever he and his wife are supposed to have sexy time?" Catherine asked.

She lowered her voice when she asked that because, no matter how much it was okay for visiting employees to gossip, limits existed in regards to acceptable topics. Yasmin pulled her head back and gasped.

"Oh, you're bad!" she said, and then giggled like a schoolgirl.

"Yeah, I bet he's like…" Catherine cleared her throat and assumed a deeper voice to mimic Lillard's. "Okay, we'll meet up here at 9 eastern standard time and we will begin with some foreplay. At 9:05 we can commence oral. Now, a little bit about oral. One issue that I always have—"

"Stop!" Yasmin exclaimed, but was red in the face, unable to contain her laughter.

She put a hand over her mouth and laughed so hard that tears streaked her face. Catherine laughed along with her. Passersby in the corridors gave them weird glances, but the women ignored them. Who cared if they were having a little juvenile fun?

The company expected them to be serious most of the time, even though they hired people as young as twenty. At least formal attire wasn't mandatory.

When Catherine and Yasmin exited the building, it was raining.

Catherine pulled her hoodie over her head, her mood instantly plummeting at the sight of the gray sky and the drizzle that fell from the clouds. The security guard opened the gate for them and let them out of the campus.

In the Seattle office, the security guard left the gate open at all times while he read the newspaper or played crossword puzzles. The one here took his job a lot more seriously. Too seriously, Catherine noticed.

Just yesterday, she left the campus during working hours in order to grab lunch with Yasmin. When they returned, the guard insisted on seeing their ID badges even though they'd been gone for only an hour.

"Hey, Wesley's hosting that gathering for engineers tonight. You wanna go?" Yasmin asked.

Catherine was tempted. It had been a while since she went out on a proper party, but at the same time, a party with engineers sounded soooooo boring.

"Pass. I'm gonna walk around town tonight a little bit. My roommate will be coming in a few days, so I want to be fresh for when she arrives."

"All right. But Paul is gonna be at the party. Just saying."

"Paul Brewer?" Catherine stopped dead in her tracks. "You mean the hot developer from the security team?"

"Uh-huh," Yasmin nodded.

She was doing it on purpose, teasing Catherine like this. She knew Catherine had the hots for Paul and that it would make her change her mind. It was working.

"How do you know about that?" Catherine asked as they continued walking side by side.

"I spoke to the others."

"Eh, it doesn't matter. Not like co-workers can hook up, anyway. It's against the company policy."

"It's against the company policy to hook up with your *teammate*. But it's not against the policy to hook up with someone outside your team." Yasmin winked.

Catherine's mouth pulled back into a smile. It was in that moment that she knew what she would be doing tonight.

"Okay, fine. Let's go to the party." She threw her hands up.

"Hell yes, girl!" Yasmin cheered.

Catherine dug through her purse and found her cellphone.

"Just going to call my roommate and see how she's doing," she said.

She dialed Melanie's phone number and listened intently to the ringing against the booming traffic. After a few rings, it went straight to voicemail. Catherine grimaced as she hung up.

"Strange. She's not answering," she said.

"Maybe she just didn't hear it." Yasmin shrugged. She must have noticed Catherine's worried gaze because she shook her shoulder and said, "Come on. I'm sure she's okay."

"Yeah," Catherine said absent-mindedly. "I mean, she does keep her phone on silent most of the time anyway."

"Right? I'm sure she'll call you as soon as she sees the missed call."

"Yeah. You're right," Catherine agreed and put the phone back in her purse. "So, what time is the party tonight?"

GAG

I awoke to a faint buzzing somewhere in the room. I knew immediately that it was my cellphone. I had hoped it was only a message because I didn't feel like getting up for a call.

It wasn't.

The vibrating was incessant and painful to my ears, like the upstairs neighbor drilling something in the early hours on a weekend. I ignored it, but the more I did so, the louder it seemed to get.

"Shut up, shut up, just shut up!" I hissed as I clasped my ears with the palms of my hands.

After what seemed like a long time, the ringing finally stopped. The silence was so beautiful. I exhaled and tried to go back to sleep. At first, it seemed as though I would fall back asleep within minutes. But then other noises started, subtle, barely perceptible, but present enough for me to hear them.

It sounded like water gently sloshing. Kind of like after you eat or drink and then lie down and then your stomach makes these weird noises. I ignored it to the best of my abilities, but the sloshing was perpetual, not giving me a moment's rest.

The more I listened to it, the less it sounded like liquid and more like–

Squelching.

I opened my eyes and listened. Millions of tiny, squirmy sounds came from deep within my stomach, my ears, my skull…

Panic should have overtaken me, but instead, all I felt was annoyance at the inability to sleep. The harder I shut my eyes and the harder I tried to ignore the sounds, the louder they became.

On cue, my stomach churned, warning me that whatever swirled in there was about to climb back out. I could no longer sleep. I rushed into the toilet, a hand clasped over my mouth. I practically dropped to my knees, gagging and retching.

And then a projectile of vomit shot out of my mouth, like a disgusting waterfall. I thought the cascade would never end and that I would choke on my own puke, but then it came to a stop, leaving me to gag, burp, and pant above the toilet.

"Fuck," I exclaimed, that feeling of fatigue creeping up on me once again.

I'd grown tired of that feeling. I just wanted to be able to live my life normally again. Another wave shot out of my mouth. I hadn't even known I could hold that much inside me, but after this wave, it must have all been gone. Although I felt better, the sickness still pervaded my entire body.

I willingly stuck a finger in my mouth and produced the gag reflex. More yellowish water riddled with chunks of food shot out of my mouth, acidic, burning my throat. I coughed and spat out the snot that hung from my lower lip.

Better. Not great, but better.

I was about to flush the toilet when my eyes fell on the contents inside it. Among the bevy of brown, smelly liquid and the chunks of food, tiny rice grains wiggled. The movement was so subtle and microscopic that I hadn't even noticed it until then. The moment I did, I retched again, but nothing came out.

Fumbling for the flush lever, I pressed down on it with a trembling hand and watched as the whirlwind in the toilet sucked everything into oblivion. I knelt there for a long moment, breathing heavily.

I could feel them squirming in my mouth. Gentle, ticklish movement on the inside of my cheeks, wedging themselves between my teeth and into my gums, crawling toward my throat and on the underside of my tongue.

My eyes fell on my reflection in the mirror. A maggot was stuck on my chin with a streak of watered-down brown, motionless. The sight of the rest of me was unbearable to watch. I don't remember what happened next.

All I know is, everything went dark.

LAB PART 5

The subject room labeled with the number 5 had a male patient, in his mid-twenties or so. It was difficult to tell because of all the rot, open wounds, and army of maggots that infested him from head to toe.

Half of his scalp was missing, eaten away by the PT-104. His eyes were completely gone, maggots squirming inside the empty sockets and burrowing into the dead flesh. Maggots poked out of his cheeks like they would out of a rotten apple. The man's collar bone was visible on display, a mess of white wormed with strings of red flesh.

Blisters covered his chest and stomach that looked bloated way out of proportions, especially considering his slim stature. Maggots slithered all over his shriveled genitals, and in and out of the urethra and foreskin.

Phillip felt his skin crawling. He wanted to scratch his own crotch just from the sight in front of him. At first, Phillip couldn't even comprehend how this person was at all still alive, let alone standing.

"What is this?" he asked, instinctively scratching the back of his hand.

He had to look down, just to make sure no maggots had somehow made it past the pane of glass and onto his skin.

"The final stage of PT-104," Simmons said. "The human specimen no longer feels a thing."

"Elaborate."

"You see, the PT-104 initially nests inside the flesh of the hosts. However, as it reproduces, it becomes impossible for it to become invisible to the host. The host, naturally, will try to remove the parasite from the body."

"Okay?"

"So, what happens is the parasite worms its way to the brain of the host. Now, we don't exactly know what happens there, but our assumption is that the parasite shuts down the nociceptors."

"You mean the host no longer feels any pain?" Phillip asked, fascinated.

"Precisely!" Simmons exclaimed, ecstatic. "But that's not all."

"Oh?"

"Not only does the host feel no more pain, but something else remarkable happens. The parasite does something in the brain to trigger a *nurturing* instinct in the host."

"What does that mean?"

"It means that the host no longer sees the parasite as a threat, but instead has the need to *protect* the parasite."

"That is incredible," Phillip said, his eyebrows raised high above his eyes.

He needed a moment to process everything Doctor Simmons had told him. How could a parasite go from being dormant in humans and utterly non-functional to becoming the super-parasite it was now?

"I wish that were the end of it, but there's more," Simmons said.

Phillip swiped a hand across his forehead. It was coated in cold sweat. Definitely not the temperature because the quarantine in the building was the coldest of them all.

"Okay. Hit me," Phillip said.

"The parasite can sense when the host's time is coming to an end. Therefore, it commands the host to spread the infection to other creatures."

"Are you saying it mind-controls the host?"

"I wouldn't go as far as to say it mind-controls it, but it does affect it enough to cause it to preserve the parasite at all costs. Think of it as *t. gondii*. The *t. gondii* infects the rat, then tells it to get eaten by a cat because the parasite can only thrive inside the cat's gut. Also, what happens to rabies. The person infected develops hydrophobia in order to have more saliva produced, therefore infecting more people and spreading. Except with PT-104, the host actively spreads the parasite!"

"Jesus Christ. This thing's a mess," Phillip said, staring at the man inside the subject room.

Maggots continually fell from his body and squirmed on the floor before regaining balance and slithering up his toes and ankles. Phillip's initial assumption was right. This was a super-parasite.

"Is that all?" Phillip asked.

He couldn't shake the feeling that Simmons still hadn't presented the main course for tonight.

"There are a few other things," Simmons replied.

"Go on."

"The PT-104... it gives remarkable strength to the host in the final stage. When it senses it's about to expire, it not only keeps the host alive by protecting the vital organs, but it also pumps insane doses of adrenaline into it, giving it inhuman strength."

"And you believe it's doing so to increase its chances of reproducing?"

"Precisely. The parasite knows the host is about to expire, and it gives it one final push to ensure it reaches a new home. The host is still aware of everything, of course, but the urge to spread the parasite is irresistible.

To us, it would look like a mindless, rabid animal exerting its violent tendencies on others, but it is actually trying to spread, even at the cost of the host's life."

"And once it has a new home, it lets the host die, correct?"

Simmons nodded.

"Anything else important I should know, Doctor Simmons?" Phillip asked.

"That's all we know," Simmons said, much to Phillip's relief.

He felt like he wouldn't be able to fall asleep for a whole week. Not with this kind of information. There was too much work to do now. He would probably need to put in a lot of overtime to learn as much as he could about the parasite, but at least the company would approve the funds for future work.

It was all thanks to Doctor Simmons. Despite being Phillip's subordinate, Phillip would allow him to take some credit for his work. Not all of it, of course, but some credit was due.

"Thank you for the good work, Doctor Simmons." Phillip put a hand on Simmons's shoulder before turning around. "You can call it a night. I'll take over from here."

"Oh, Doctor Curtis?" Simmons called out. "There is only one more thing I forgot to mention."

"And what's that?" Phillip turned around.

Simmons grinned. He looked like he was having a hard time staving off laughter.

"The parasite is no longer contained," he said.

SCRATCH SCRATCH SCRATCH

The squelching was what woke me up. It came to me while I was still unconscious, barely audible, as if through a long tunnel. Then it gradually got closer and closer until it was directly in my ear, not only producing the sound, but tickling my earlobe.

I opened my eyes and stared at the maggot-infested bathroom floor. The tickling inched toward my eardrum. Even if I had the strength, I wouldn't bother stopping it. What was the point? I could feel and hear the maggot crawling into my ear. The sound was amplified, so much that I could hear every wet slithering sound it made, coupled with loud sucking that must have come from its mute mouth.

The intensity of the noise could be compared to someone wrinkling a piece of paper right next to your ear.

It took me a long time to move a muscle. The tickling wasn't just in my ear, I realized. It was all over my body, my face, inside my clothes…

I clambered up to my feet – even doing that seemed to drain a lot of energy from me – and looked in the mirror. No reaction would have been an exaggerated one at the sight in front of me. Screaming, crying, smashing the mirror… none of that would be enough to convey the horror that I saw.

The first thing that caught my eye was the myriad of maggots all over my hair, face, neck, and clothes. They crawled in random directions, some of them falling off and plopping on the bathroom floor. I looked like I had confetti all over me.

A patch of black covered my forehead. I could see the tiny tip of something yellow wiggling until it burrowed deeper. One clung to my lower lip and crawled into my mouth. It was faster than I expected. One moment it was there, the next – gone.

The red cold-sore-like blister that adorned the corner of my lip earlier was now a divot filled with pus and rotted flesh. Black patches and spots covered my neck and shoulders, almost making me look like a Dalmatian dog.

I leaned closer to the mirror. The arteries in my eyes had strained and popped, making my eyeballs look bloodshot. Just under the thin veil of white, next to my pupil, I thought I saw a grain firmly stuck on the inside. Something tickled my lower eyelid.

The blisters on my chest were larger and more swollen. They were itchy, so itchy. The sensation was unbearable. I raised a hand to one of them and gently scratched. The blister felt like a balloon filled with water. It felt good to scratch, but not enough. It only made the itch shift deeper.

I scratched harder. The blister dipped under my touch. I scratched and scratched and scratched. It felt really good. Better than an orgasm. But it still wasn't enough. I had been using the tips of my blackened fingers to scratch up until then.

Now, I dug my broken nails into the blister and pressed hard. The watery mass beneath slipped under the pressure of my nails. The itch was deeper and I had to get to it. Nothing else mattered.

Not the crawling sensation all over my body, not the rot that pervaded my skin, just the itch. I clawed and raked at the blister, each time pressing harder, leaving scratch marks all over my skin, and then–

A hollow pop as the blister exploded, firing pus, blood, and maggots in a downward projectile that slid down my torso. With the watery mass deflated, I could reach the itch easier. It still wasn't enough. I scratched with more intensity.

The blister flaked off until all that remained instead of it was a deep crater. I didn't stop scratching. My black fingers were coated with pus, blood, and minced maggots that were unlucky enough to get in contact with my nails.

The itch was still there. It was under the other blisters as well. I used both hands and raked them incessantly, frustrated, growling in annoyance. I needed a tool. Yes, that was it. I needed something that would be able to scratch deeper.

I rushed into the kitchen and grabbed a fork. It was not wide enough, but it would have to do. Pressing it against my itchy skin and pulling down felt so, so good. The sensation was so pleasant that I had to throw my head back and moan in pleasure.

The smaller blisters refused to pop, so I punctured them with the fork and squeezed the pus and the maggots out. My chest was a fleshy mess of holes, but the itch was finally allaying. I dropped the fork on the floor – its tines were stained with various colors and tissues – and breathed a sigh of relief.

My stomach rumbled, protesting in hunger. I put my palm on it, as if to soothe it. There had to be some food in the apartment. I walked to the fridge and opened it. A plethora of food sat inside – yogurts, puddings, vegetables, dried meat, dairy products and more.

I grabbed the jar of peanut butter and yanked it out with feverish hands. I unscrewed the lid and the smell of peanut immediately wafted to my face, making me gag.

On a whim, I chucked it across the room. The jar fell on the floor and rolled over to the other side of the room.

It didn't break, which was frustrating, but I had more pressing matters to worry about. Rifling through the contents of the fridge, I found nothing appetizing. The smell of all the food made me feel sick, and yet I had to eat something.

My body required something different.

I opened the freezer and dug through the frozen pizzas, vegetables, and pies. My eyes fell on the beef. I pulled it out, unwrapped it, put it on a plate, and then tossed it in the microwave.

The timer on the microwave ticked slowly, too slowly. I watched as my meal rotated under the interior light, defrosting. Thirty seconds wasn't enough, so I reset the timer. I couldn't wait any longer.

I opened the microwave while five seconds still remained and pulled the plate out. If it was hot, I couldn't feel it. The smell of raw beef invaded my nostrils. It caused my mouth to water. I hadn't felt like that since having my first reward meal after finishing a strict diet.

I licked my lips – something was on them, a maggot, I assumed – and took the piece of raw meat into my hands. I ravenously bit into it. It was beautifully tough and caused my teeth to sink into it like mud. The exterior was hot, and the interior icy. I bit as hard as I could and tore a chunk, the savory taste of raw meat filling my mouth.

I chewed with impatient complacence before gulping the large piece. I bit down again, but couldn't bite through. I unclenched my jaw and took a smaller bite. I noticed that one of my teeth was left embedded in the meat where I had bitten earlier.

That didn't stop me from taking the next bite. The broken-off tooth along with the meat swam in my mouth, ground against my good teeth – I noticed that some of them were unsteady in their roots – until I spat it out.

The beef was gone before long, every last bite of it swallowed. My gaze fell on the plate where the blood swam. I brought the plate up to my mouth and gulped the blood. It was the most delicious juice I'd ever had.

I needed more.

More meat sat in the freezer. The thought of having to wait for all of them to defrost was unnerving. I took out all the meat products and let them defrost while putting a steak into the microwave.

This time, I didn't even wait for it to defrost properly. The hard, icy meat hurt my teeth and gums, but I didn't care. Bite after bite, I ate the steak until it, too, was gone. I wiped my mouth with my forearm and let out another sigh of pleasure.

That must have been the best meal I'd ever had.

My moment of buoyance was interrupted by a loud buzzing. My head snapped in the direction of the coffee table where my phone was vibrating, the screen lit up. I ambled toward it sleepily and picked it up.

It was Darren.

I accepted the call and pressed the phone up to my ear – the one where the maggot wasn't nestled. I heard nothing at first, and then a familiar male voice.

"Hello? Melanie?" Darren asked.

"Yes," I said.

"Hey, it's Darren," he said jovially.

"I know," I coldly replied.

"How have you been? Been a while since I heard your voice."

"Fine."

That lack of proper interaction seemed to extinguish his buoyance immediately.

"Okay… hey, listen," he said. "I'm back in Seattle. My business trip was cut short. I guess they didn't see the point in trying to convince a bunch of old doofuses on a new-age deal."

He chuckled. I remained silent. Darren cleared his throat, audibly uncomfortable.

"I was wondering… are you by any chance free tonight?" he asked. When I didn't respond, he added, "I know it's sudden and all, but I kind of wanted to see you, and–"

"Come to my place," I said.

Darren must have been taken by surprise because he didn't say anything for a long moment.

"You want me to come to your place?" he asked.

"Yes," I said.

"Oh. Cool. What time works for you?"

"Now."

"Now?"

"Yes."

I quickly recited my address to him.

"Oh. Okay. Cool, I'll be there in, uh, about twenty minutes. Is that okay?" he asked.

"Yes. See you," I said and hung up.

VISIT

Darren found the phone call with Melanie a little strange. She might have been tired or something, he figured, or maybe he woke her up from a nap. She mentioned sometimes taking naps in the afternoon.

But it's 7 pm, he realized.

So what? His ex used to take naps at 8 pm, only to wake up at 11, have a meal, and go right back to bed. He had been looking forward to seeing Melanie his whole business trip. He thought about her daily. In fact, he wanted to call her, just to hear her voice, but he didn't want to come off as too needy.

You're already falling in love, Darren, buddy.

Nope, that was wrong. He *was already* in love with Melanie. He hated being so emotional and getting attached to people so easily. It always ended up with him getting dumped by the girl.

Ever since his last relationship where he went all in and ended up getting dumped for a biker, he decided not to be so hasty in the future. Truth be told, he wanted to kiss Melanie the night they went out on a date in the park, but he didn't want to blow his chances with her by being pushy.

Then the stupid business trip came up and he had to postpone their next date. If it hadn't been for that, they might have been dating already. Darren often fantasized about Melanie as his girlfriend.

He loved everything about her. The way she shyly laughed when she told jokes, the way she looked when she wore baggy clothes, the way she smiled, the tone of her voice…

The great looks were only a huge plus. And on top of that, it felt good thinking about bragging that he had a girlfriend who's a software engineer.

Darren stopped at a flower shop and bought a bouquet of roses on his way to Melanie's apartment. The closer he got, the more nervous he became. This would be the first time they spent time alone in a private place.

He wondered if her intention for calling him over was what he thought it was. That caused butterflies in his stomach to go wild. Darren didn't care if they would sleep or not – although that would be one mind-blowing experience.

But one thing was for sure, though. Darren would kiss her tonight. He would stop being a coward and holding his emotions in check. He would kiss her and reveal his true emotions to Melanie.

He wouldn't tell her that he loved her, no. That would be a little too much and too fast.

It took everything inside Darren not to run the red lights in order to reach Melanie sooner. Once he was in front of her apartment building, a shiver enveloped him. He was both nervous and excited at the same time.

He got out of the car, the bouquet in his hand. He rang the intercom for Melanie's apartment and the door buzzed open. He stepped inside and climbed up to the floor where she lived. In the vacant corridor of the building, he heard just how heavy his breathing was.

Calm down, Darren. You're here to kiss the girl you like, not ask her to marry you.

That self-pep-talk didn't make him feel any better. He walked up to the door and rang the bell. That moment between the bell ringing and the door opening was the worst. It was always filled with nerve-wracking silence and anticipation.

Darren cleared his throat and ran a hand through his hair. He hoped that his breath didn't smell bad. The lock of the door clicked. Darren assumed a firmer composure.

The door never opened.

Darren squinted, and then waited a little longer. The doorknob rattled and the door opened a crack. The door was going to swing aside any moment now and Melanie would be standing there, as beautiful as ever.

But that never happened.

Darren didn't want to intrude, but then he realized that the door probably opened exactly because Melanie was inviting him in. She might be wearing some sexy lingerie and waiting for him in the bedroom in that very moment.

That was enough for him to make the decision.

He pushed the door open. It creaked and revealed the dark interior of the foyer.

"Hello? Mel?" he asked as he stepped inside.

The apartment was quiet. Darren squinted against the dark, trying to make out where the light switch was.

"In here," a soft voice said from a nearby room.

A smile crept on Darren's face. He put the flowers on the counter and walked toward the sound of her voice. His shin bumped into something. He yowled and regained his composure, approaching the bedroom.

The lights were all off and he didn't want to turn them on and ruin Melanie's romantic atmosphere.

"Come in here," Melanie said just as Darren approached the half-open bedroom door.

Darren pushed the door open and stepped inside. He hadn't realized until then, but the smile had been fixed on his face. This was really happening!

The room was dark, but his eyes detected Melanie's silhouette on the bed. She was lying sideways, as if on a beach, and Darren could see the beautiful features of her naked body.

His breath caught.

Melanie beckoned him over with words he didn't understand because he was so focused on her. He took steps toward her, giddy with excitement. She stood up in front of him. As she pressed against him, he could tell that he was right – she was naked.

He felt her fingers brushing the nape of his neck. His insides were melting. He could no longer take it. He leaned toward her and kissed her. Their lips touching felt so electrical.

How many times had he imagined kissing those lips, trying to decipher what they would taste like? Now, it was actually happening.

It was a gentle peck, but then he became more daring, smooched her and then explored her mouth. The tips of her fingers tickled his neck and his ears. She ran a hand down his chest. She opened her mouth to embrace him in a deeper kiss.

Her breath hit him like a truck. It was putrid, like hot garbage that had been left out in the sun for too long. He tried not to recoil, but he felt his eyes watering up. Okay, so she might have had a rotten tooth. No big deal.

She kissed him, and he kissed her back, their tongues exploring each other. The metallic smell and taste were becoming unbearable. Melanie had beautiful teeth, he never would have thought her breath smelled like this.

Something was wrong.

The tickling on the nape of his neck slithered down the collar of his shirt where it continued to descend. His hand had reached for her chest and the fingertips touched something wet. Darren pulled back, a moment of respite that he so desperately needed.

Nothing about this was romantic anymore. All that remained in Darren was a squirming, crawling sensation that begged him to get away from Melanie.

Something tickled his lip. His hand swatted at it. Something mushy came off. He knew right away that it was a bug because he felt its meticulous movement.

"What the hell?" Darren asked, the tickling and itchy feeling now all over his body.

He strode to the light switch and flipped it on. Melanie had remained entrenched in her spot when he looked at her.

For a very long moment, he was sure that this was just a terrible – but very realistic – costume prank, because there was no way in hell something as repulsive as the thing that stood before him could be real.

Melanie was entirely naked in front of him. Her hair disheveled and straw-like, tufts of it ripped from their roots, revealing a bloodied skull. Her eye was a bloodied soup-like cavity, a home for a cluster of maggots that wiggled inside. Her skin was a fleshy mess dotted with black spots, flaking skin, and blisters.

Maggots crawled into every orifice of her being, going in and out as they pleased while Melanie stood perfectly calm, as if the thing before him was an entity created from the maggots themselves. Her arm – the one that had been bitten by the dog, Darren remembered – was chewed all the way to the bone, showing sinew and cartilage on the meat that remained.

A tickle inside Darren's mouth caused him to spit on the floor with a never-before exerted propulsion.

When he looked at the floor, he saw a tiny maggot in the spit. He screamed at the realization that they were all over his body. He swatted at his face, his hair, his neck, his hands, and stormed out of the room while yanking his shirt off.

The last he saw of Melanie was the reticent stare she gave him with the remaining eye as he ran outside, stripping out of his clothes until he was only in his underwear.

TRIP

"Come on, I'm sure she's okay," Yasmin said to a worried Catherine.

Catherine paid no attention to her. As indifferent as Catherine was about things, Yasmin was like that even more so – but only when it came to the troubles of others. If it was something of her own, she'd be all over it in minutes.

"She's still not answering her phone…" Catherine said as she lowered the cellphone from her ear, biting her nails and staring at the glowing screen.

She and Yasmin were at the hotel booked by the company. In a couple of days, they would check out because the trip would be officially over. Catherine's ticket back to Seattle was booked at a later time, but now that things were so dire, she would need to go back home sooner.

Melanie hadn't answered her phone in days. Not only that, but no response to Catherine's messages, either. She was always online on social media, at least during work hours, because her team had a group chat there.

Something was wrong. As much as Catherine's brain scrambled to convince itself it was just a misunderstanding – because bad things don't happen to someone you know, they only happen to people on the news who you've never heard about – she knew she couldn't ignore such red flags.

"I'm going back," she said as she shot up to her feet.

"What?" Yasmin raised her eyebrows. "Wait, you're going back to Seattle? Tonight? But we're still not done with the business conference."

Catherine was already stuffing her clothes into the suitcase. Yasmin continued spewing words about how she shouldn't leave now and that she was overreacting, but she wasn't paying much attention. The only thought that loomed above her head like a black cloud was whether Melanie was okay.

"Catherine, at least call the police and tell them to do a welfare check before you go," Yasmin said, exasperation lacing her voice.

She probably noticed that she wouldn't be able to talk Catherine out of leaving. It never took long for people to realize just how stubborn Catherine was. Whenever someone gave her a piece of advice, she did the opposite. She still didn't know why she did it, but she did. Maybe she hated being ordered around?

Only her ex-boyfriend Caleb knew how to handle her. Whenever she asked for advice – specifically about fitness and nutrition, since he was a coach – he would tell her what to do, and she would find an excuse not to do it.

Caleb would then shrug and tell her, sure, she can do it how she wants. That lack of interest worked as well as reverse psychology and drew Catherine in – made her actually listen to Caleb here and there.

"Good idea," Catherine said. "I'll call the police on my way back to Seattle."

"Cat…" Yasmin sighed.

"Sorry, Yasmin. I have to go. Something's wrong with my roommate and I can't ignore it anymore. What if she had an accident at home and can't move?"

That thought caused a shiver to surge through Catherine's body like an electrical current. Her vivid mind imagined Melanie laying on the kitchen floor, her limbs splayed in random directions, the back of her skull bleeding onto the tiled floor in an ever-expanding pool.

Catherine packed even faster.

Yasmin had given up by then on trying to convince her to stay. Instead, she helped Catherine pack and made a call to book a last-minute flight ticket. She then called a taxi for her. Catherine was ready to leave within minutes.

"Please be careful, Cat," Yasmin said as they stood at the door.

Catherine had two suitcases in her hands, a thick jacket filled with important documents, and a scarf that enveloped her neck. Just minutes ago, she was in her pajamas, sitting on the bed and getting ready to call it a night. The whole thing brought a sense of urgency in her – something that told her she needed to be even faster.

"I'll be fine," Catherine said. "It's Melanie I'm worried about."

Yasmin looked like she was about to start crying. Her lip quivered and the corners of her eyebrows arched as she lunged to embrace Catherine in a bear hug.

"Come on, it's not like we'll never see each other again," Catherine said. "You'll be back at the office in a bit, anyway."

"I know. It's just… there was so much we should have done together!" Yasmin's voice cracked.

Catherine's hands were occupied with luggage, so she couldn't pat Yasmin on the back even if she wanted to – which she didn't. Standing at the door while having Yasmin hugging her and shuddering was only making her irritable. It was the equivalent of having to console her Aunt Betty who became overly emotional at every family gathering.

When Yasmin finally pulled back, she wiped the tears off her face and wished Catherine luck. Catherine flashed her a sour smile, something that mutely said "Thanks, I guess."

And then she was on her way back home.

As soon as she was inside the taxi, she told the driver where to take her and whipped out her phone. She wondered if she had forgotten to bring anything important and hoped that wasn't the case. If she left anything at the hotel, Yasmin could scoop it up for her.

She dialed emergency services and pressed the phone to her ear. After a short moment, the operator answered. The conversation itself was a blur for Catherine. All she knew was that the police agreed to send out a patrol to the address in order to check on Melanie. Catherine thanked them and hung up before continuing to bite her nails, waiting for the taxi to break through the incessant traffic and reach the airport.

OVERTAKE

I felt no pain. In fact, I felt better than I have my entire life. I was powerful, I was strong. I could do anything with my new body. This wasn't a disease. It was a gift. I don't know where the time went after Darren left.

It could have been day or night, I had no idea. When I looked down at one point, I noticed that I was missing a finger. My entire hand was black by then all the way to the wrist, and my ring finger was missing, a diagonal stump with a sharp piece of bone protruding out.

It didn't bother me at all. I ate more meat after Darren left. I had to feed my babies. The ones that had been swirling inside me, swimming in my flesh, in my skull, in my eyes, ears, and mouth. I had to feed to keep them strong.

I didn't feel the hunger anymore. I just ate on an instinct for my children. I thought I heard knocking and ringing somewhere, but I was far too busy to bother with it. When I looked down again, a huge hole decorated my thigh. I could see the femur where the maggots feasted, and the rot that coated the bloodied wound.

I flexed my quadriceps but nothing happened. I could still stand on that leg, but it moved funny. I needed more meat. I had already eaten everything from the freezer and needed more.

Was that knocking I heard? Ringing? I couldn't hear well from the squirming in my ears. It was irrelevant. Everything was a blur anyway. All I could hear was my babies feasting.

Then a deep, booming voice came, snapping me out of my stupor.

"This is the police. Is anybody home?"

I froze. They were here to take my children away. Someone told them about my children. The guy who stopped by earlier must have done it. The one I used to date. Dammit, what was his name? I couldn't remember his name. Even his face was a blur.

I remembered his look of terror as he stormed out, half-naked, but it all felt like it had happened hundreds of years ago. Three loud knocks reminded me that the visitors were still at the door.

"Ma'am, are you home? We're coming in!" the voice said.

I had to act fast. My senses sharpened. My body became tense like an arrow. I ran to the kitchen counter and grabbed a knife before retreating to the bathroom. I held the knife with both hands – I had to readjust my grip because my nerves no longer functioned in my fingers, and my fingertips had been nibbled to the bone.

As if on cue, the squirming inside my skull ceased, letting me listen more intently to the intruders at the door. I listened as the creaking of the door came from the entrance, followed by hollow thuds. Someone calling my name, then heavy footsteps.

"Ma'am? Anybody home?" one of the voices asked.

"Jesus, what the hell is this?" another voice, who I assumed was the partner of the intruder, asked.

"What? Oh, crap. Are those maggots?"

"And what's that smell? Holy Christ. Smells like shit. We might be dealing with a stiff here."

"Yeah. Let's check it out."

I listened as the footsteps intermittently receded and grew louder from the policemen inspecting my apartment. They commented about how dirty and smelly the apartment was. Then one of them said, "I'm gonna take a look over there."

I heard the footsteps separating. The squirming inside my body intensified at the intruder approaching the bathroom.

Patience, my darlings. I'll keep you safe from the bad men.

I pressed my back against the wall and held the knife firmly in my hands. I stared at the door, waiting for it to open. The footsteps approached, then stopped. They were right in front of the door now. My eyes –eye, actually – fell on the shadow under the door.

The doorknob turned. The door opened with a creak.

The moment the head poked through the door, my blade swung downward. The tip of the kitchen knife went through the police officer's temple, just behind the eye. It penetrated the skull with a lot more ease than I thought it would. My babies must have given me the strength I needed to protect them.

The cop never even saw it coming. His eyes were fixated on the sink in front, but the moment the blade struck him, his gaze widened, a gentle trickle of blood running down the spot where he'd been stabbed. He limply fell headlong a moment later, the blade still stuck in his head.

"Wheeler?" the other policeman said.

He had heard it and now he was going to come inspect what happened to his partner. I was ready. I pulled out the knife and braced myself for the other intruder.

"Holy fuck!" he exclaimed, most likely when he laid eyes on the feet of his dead partner sticking out of the bathroom.

"Come out with your hands in the air!" the cop said.

I happily obliged. I stepped over the dead police officer and came into view, the knife firm in my hand. The police officer was young, maybe around my age. When he saw me, the barrel of his gun shook. His eyeballs grew so wide that I thought they were going to pop out of his skull.

"Holy shit," he said as he took a step back. "Stay back. Stay the fuck back!"

I didn't stay back. In fact, I took a step forward. The cop backpedaled. I jackknifed toward him. He took another step back. His finger was on the trigger, itching to fire, but for some reason, no shots came just yet. Perhaps he was a rookie who had never shot someone before.

Perhaps he didn't want the blood of another human being on his hands, even if it meant losing his own life.

Or maybe he knew killing me would be wrong. Maybe he saw the sheer beauty of me and my children and knew that killing us would be the wrong thing to do.

Whatever it was, the police officer never had the chance to think it through because, when he took another step backward, he tripped on the coffee table and fell on his back, smashing his head on the floor.

His look of terror immediately morphed into stupor and confusion, his eyes wandering in random directions, like a drunken person's would. I was already on top of him, my babies falling all over him and wiggling into his clothes, climbing into his orifices, dropping into his mouth as he tried to scream.

I brought the knife down on the officer's chest. He yelped. A red splotch covered his uniform. I pulled the knife out and brought it down again, and again, over and over until his face went limp and he no longer moved.

I should have been exhausted, but I felt great. I felt like I could run fifty miles. I got closer to the officer's face and opened my mouth against his. Maggots slithered against my tongue and the inside of my mouth, carried by the salty saliva, passing onto the police officer.

When I moved away, already, I could see them burrowing inside his skin until they were completely inside, leaving minuscule red dots as the only evidence of ever entering. They would continue to feast on his flesh. It would not keep them fed for long, but it would make a good snack.

I needed something living for them to thrive. I didn't have much time left, I knew that much. I needed to get them to a better home if I had any hope for them to survive.

LAB PART 6

"What?" Phillip asked.

Simmons's face was slack, for the first time that night, Phillip noticed. If Phillip didn't know him any better, he would have thought Simmons looked like an action movie villain.

"Oh, don't worry. It's not like it was an accident or anything like that," Simmons said with a shrug.

Phillip didn't like this one bit. He didn't like the smug look on Simmons' face, either. He knew that Simmons hated working as Phillip's subordinate – especially that his superior was Phillip himself.

He had made that clear since day one.

Although he couldn't openly disagree or defy Phillip, Simmons made sure to poke and prod from time to time, occasionally mentioning how he had more expertise. It was the truth. Simmons had more experience, but the company chose Phillip for the position of lead scientist because he had demonstrated better skills. It goes to show that having a fancy degree means nothing.

The worst thing must have been the fact that both Simmons and Phillip applied for the same position at the same time, which effectively made them rivals. Phillip never wanted a rivalry with someone like Simmons, especially since he could learn so much from a man like him, but Simmons didn't seem to want to bury the hatchet.

Eventually, Phillip started treating Simmons the way he treated the rest of the scientists on the team – no exemptions, and especially no tolerance toward ignoring the superior's orders and doing things his own way.

Simmons never liked that.

"Well, then tell me what happened! How did a parasite this deadly managed to get out of containment? Speak!" Phillip insisted.

Simmons flashed him an enigmatic smile. What did it mean? Did Simmons allow the parasite to escape? He knew that if anything went wrong or the microorganisms found their way out of quarantine, it would be Phillip's job on the line.

That was the shitty thing about being a lead scientist or lead anything at any work. Whenever something went wrong, it was always the person in charge getting blamed. Could it be that Simmons did this on purpose to get Phillip fired so that he could step in and take the role of the lead scientist?

No, that would never work. The company monitored everything. They would know that Simmons did things behind Phillip's back and that he was the one responsible for unleashing the parasite. It would take a while, and Phillip would most likely be suspended for the time being, but in the end, his name would be cleared, and he would be able to return to work, compensated for the wrongful suspension.

"The company allowed it to get out," Simmons finally said, stopping all those crazy thoughts in Phillip's head dead in their tracks.

"What?!" Phillip exclaimed. "The company allowed it?! I don't believe you."

"Come with me. I'll show you," Simmons said.

They walked out of quarantine, leaving the patients in their cells. Phillip couldn't get to the office fast enough. He was eager to see what it was that Simmons wanted to show him.

Every time a big decision was made, like the one now – where the parasite would be released into the wild – the scientists had to get approval from the higher-ups. It was a long and tedious process that required tons of paperwork, approvals, appeals, and so on.

They left the quarantine, walked across the corridor and entered the administration area. Phillip spent a lot of time in this section, especially before and after each experiment started.

Simmons went to his desk and rummaged through the drawer.

"Let's see here… Ah, here it is," Simmons said as he pulled out a folder and presented it to Phillip with a conniving grin.

Phillip snatched the folder out of Simmons' hand and skimmed through the papers. Sure enough, no matter how many times he overturned the pages, the big red stamp with the letters APPROVED stood in his face. It was a one-of-a-kind stamp, and no way could it be forged.

"They approved the canine specimen infected with the PT-104 to be released into the city? Are they out of their minds?! Who petitioned for this?!" Phillip demanded, waving the papers in front of Simmons' face.

"I did. You see, we didn't just find a way to evolve the parasite. We also found a cure," Simmons calmly said.

"A cure?!" Phillip asked in disbelief.

"Yes. A very simple one in the form of a pill. Pop the pill, and the parasite is reverse-engineered."

"What are you talking about?"

"Read the files, Doctor Curtis."

Phillip did as Simmons asked. On one of the pages, there were pictures of a patient in the final stages of the parasitic overtake, half-rotted, missing both arms and eyes, a cavity in the middle of its chest where a school of maggots nested. The next page showed the same patient, healthy, all parts of its body restored. Phillip darted his eyes across each line of the report.

"Regenerative abilities?" he asked.

"Indeed. One pill is enough to reverse engineer the parasite. Instead of feasting on the body, it regenerates it. Everything, including the bone and muscle tissue is restored in a matter of weeks. Imagine the possibilities! If someone is missing an arm, all we need to do is infect them, give them the pill, and they will be as good as new. If someone has back problems, knee problems, sight problems, a cancer, anything! All of it can be cured with the PT-104."

Phillip stared at the report papers, dumbstruck. Here, they were trying to engineer a parasite into becoming the ultimate bio weapon, wasting months and months of their time, and now Doctor Simmons managed to create not just a deadly bio weapon, but a cure for practically everything that ever existed?

Remarkable, he wanted to say, but he didn't want to let Simmons know that he was impressed, even though Simmons could probably already see it.

"I don't understand the endgame."

"It's simple. The parasite is a piggybank. It won't work well as a weapon, but what we will do is wait for the disease to spread, panic to overtake the world, and then the company will come out of the shadows and present its miracle pill as a solution. The world will flock to buy it, ensuring funds for far more ambitious experiments."

"And this has all been tested already? Both the parasite and the cure?" Phillip asked.

"Yes. They wouldn't have approved my request without having concrete evidence, first."

146

My request. That made Phillip angry. *He* was the lead scientist, not Simmons, but Simmons' ego got the better of him and he decided to take the lead.

"You went behind my back, you did extra experimentation, and you released the parasite without consulting me first?!" Phillip asked, squeezing the paper in his hand so much that it crumpled.

"I was going to consult you, Doctor Curtis, but some things have changed in the meantime."

"What things? Speak up!" Phillip practically yelled at this point.

"When I went to appeal to the committee about the parasite, they didn't want to hear it at first. But then when I produced these ground-breaking results, they changed their minds. They were very happy."

The doors opened and four armed security guards strode inside.

"In fact, they were so happy that they decided to appoint me as the lead scientist," Simmons said.

"What is this?" Phillip asked as the guards stopped inches in front of him, surrounding him.

Simmons got so close to Phillip that the faint smell of mint wafted into his face. Simmons always loved chewing mint while they weren't in quarantine.

"You're out of the picture, Curtis," Simmons said. He had never called him Curtis before. It was either "Doctor" or "Doctor Curtis."

"What did you do?" Phillip asked.

"The committee knows you're incompetent. They know this is the third experiment in a row where you failed to produce results. They planned on firing you, but I told them not to do it. I told them you can still help the company's experiments. I told them to reserve the cell number six for you because that's your daughter's age right now and you won't get to see her anymore."

Phillip jostled past Simmons, but what chance did he stand? He was just a scientist surrounded by four armed and trained security guards. Was it a surprise that they managed to subdue him with ease?

"You son of a bitch! Don't do this!" Phillip screamed. "You can't do this to me! I'm Doctor Curtis! Let me go!"

The last thing Doctor Phillip Curtis saw before getting dragged out of the office and toward the quarantine was Doctor Simmons smelling a Cuban cigar – a cigar from Phillip's personal stash.

HOMECOMING

When Catherine arrived at her apartment building, she froze. For a moment, she couldn't believe whether what she was seeing was real or not. The entire building was wrapped in a layer of something that looked like a ginormous plastic bag – including the windows and all. In Catherine's mind, it looked like a giant building wrapped as a present. The only thing it was missing was a bow tie.

In front of the building, figures dressed from head to toe in blue clothes and wearing gas masks buzzed left and right. The police and ambulance stood further away, just beyond the fence they had erected to stop trespassers from entering.

Catherine's first thought was – something happened to Melanie. She dashed forward but was quickly apprehended by a police officer.

"Ma'am, you can't go in there!" he said as he firmly held her by the wrists.

"I live here!" Catherine protested.

"Ma'am, please. It's dangerous."

Dangerous?!

"My roommate! She's in there!" Catherine insisted.

"The building is quarantined. There's a dangerous disease inside. You can't go inside."

"But my roommate–"

"Look, the CDC has been called on-site, that's how serious it is. You have to stay put, or I'm going to arrest you for interfering."

Catherine knew she had no choice but to wait. Jesus, what the hell was going on? A dangerous disease? Did one of the tenants get sick with something infectious?

Did Melanie get infected?

It all came rushing back to her like slide reels played on a projector. The dog bite. The pain in the wound. The inability to have it heal. The dog bite. The dog bite. The dog bite.

Shit, it's Melanie. She contracted something bad.

"Uh, excuse me? Officer?" Catherine called out to the cop.

He turned to face her.

"My roommate. Her name is Melanie. She's been bitten by a dog a few weeks ago. Is that the reason why the CDC is here?"

"A dog, you say? Where?"

"Some park, I don't know."

The cop looked like he wasn't about to take her seriously. Whether it was genuine concern or courtesy, he told her to wait while he went to speak to the hazmat-suited figures in front.

People had gathered around the building. Passersby were curious about what was going on. It was concert-crowded. Catherine pushed through the crowd to try and take a better look at the building.

Screams and gasps erupted from the throng just as Catherine pushed her way through, exclaiming "excuse me" and "sorry" along the way.

A figure emerged from the front entrance. It took the CDC staff a moment to notice her. In the dark, Catherine couldn't recognize her either, save for the sickly slim stature. And then Melanie stepped out into the light and Catherine felt her throat constricting. She wanted to scream, but her voice was lost.

Melanie stood in plain sight, completely naked, her body covered in patches of rot, holes, and craters. Her scalp was half-flayed, her eye devoured entirely. Tiny grains fell out of the holes in her body, and only when she got closer, Catherine saw that those grains were actually maggots.

Someone in the crowd retched while the rest of the group dispersed. Some held their phones up to film the whole thing. CDC members were around Melanie, trying to calm her down and tell her to go back inside while cops told the people to disperse – their voices fell on deaf ears.

"Ma'am! Get back insi–" one of the CDC guys yelled, but Melanie lunged at him with inhuman speed.

She was on top of him, and before Catherine could process what was going on, the CDC member's mask had been yanked off. Melanie puked in his face, a brown and red liquid riddled with those same, tiny grains.

The rest of the members subdued Melanie. Her stomach was bloated, covered with blue veins that wormed on the skin. It looked like it was about to–

Melanie's stomach burst with a popping sound, a bevy of maggots crawled out, slithering across the floor and reaching the crowd. The screams intensified and the crowd pushed to get out, elbowing and kicking Catherine.

Catherine didn't want to stay a moment longer, either. She'd seen enough. Whatever that worm-infested thing in front of the apartment was, it was no longer her roommate. Catherine wanted to erase that image from her head and pretend she never saw it, pretend Melanie never existed.

"Fuck! It got inside my ear!" someone shouted.

People squirmed and batted each other, some even stripping out of their clothes. Catherine knew it was futile. She might have gotten some inside of her, too. Touching everything suddenly seemed so, so wrong.

Only when she made it out of the crowd did she stop and turn around, breathless, sweaty, unable to inhale. The CDC members were in front of the building, surrounding a now-motionless Melanie.

RENEWAL

"How are you feeling?" Doctor Regina Weaver asked me.

"My answer hasn't changed since two hours ago, doc," I said as I theatrically rolled my eyes.

I wanted them to know how annoyed I was. I knew my juvenile tantrums wouldn't play a factor in whether they would release me earlier or not, but I still wanted them to know I didn't appreciate being treated as a lab rat.

"Any pains?" Regina asked.

She insisted I call her Regina. I think it was just her way of trying to build rapport with me.

"Nope," I said.

"In your fingers? Your abdomen? Scalp? Eye?" Regina listed.

I shook my head to all those questions. Regina nodded. She didn't bring her notepad anymore. For the first two weeks she kept taking notes like I was inside the shrink's office, but later on she dismissed her staff and just talked one on one with me.

She was pleasant to talk to. She was maybe a few years older than me, but a lot smarter and more experienced in life. The creases on her face served as testament to the bad things she's seen in life.

From what I was able to gather during our talks, Regina was married for a few years and had a son in middle school. She didn't talk a lot about herself. I was just able to figure out that info from when she occasionally slipped during our conversations.

"How's your eyesight?" she asked.

"As good as new," I said. "In fact, I think I see better on that eye now. When I wear glasses, I can see a difference."

"Yeah, that's what the reverse-engineered parasite does. It regenerates the cells not just to their original state, but also makes them better."

"Tell me about it. I used to have problems with my back all the time at work. Now I can bend in all kinds of shapes. Maybe I should let those maggots eat my other eye, too."

The doctor didn't find the zinger funny. She put her hands in the pockets of her lab coat and smiled. I think that was the first time I've seen her smile. I also remember thinking how she should smile more often because the expression made her look beautiful.

"Well, I have some good news, Melanie. You get to go home tomorrow," she said.

"Would you mind repeating that? The maggot in my ear is chewing too loud," I said.

Over the last few months, I had developed a sardonic sense of humor – one which I never knew I was capable of. How I arrived at the hospital is a blur for me.

I remember being in my apartment and I remember thinking how it was totally okay to rot the way I did and to have the maggots inside my body – just thinking about that makes my skin crawl! – but then the rest fades into nothingness.

The next thing I remember is waking up in the hospital, bandaged, stuck in a room barred with plexiglass, unable to move, talk, or see out of my eye, with a blurry vision in the other. People in lab coats were on the other side of the glass, taking notes and taking amongst each other as if I were an animal on display in the zoo.

I faded in and out of consciousness after that. Then one day, I regained my consciousness to see what a mangled mess I was. Instead of a hand I had a stump with a bloodied bandage covering it, my skin was sallow and riddled with holes. I was also missing a few toes.

The doctors had to give me sedatives to stop my screaming. Over the next few weeks, I recovered. I got used to the fact that I would never be able to use my hand properly again, but then, miraculously, I started to notice my stump growing. It kept on growing until I had my hand and fingers back, fully functional.

The rest of my wounds had healed as well, including my eye. The doctors were still apprehensive around me. They wore full protective suits and refused to make any contact with me unless it was through thick, astronaut-like gloves.

I couldn't tell how much time had passed, but I had fully recovered and demanded to be let go, but the doctors refused to answer any of my questions. One day, Catherine came to visit me. Words can't describe how happy I was to see her.

The doctors allowed us to hug and we had a heartfelt greeting where we both cried our eyes out. Doctor Regina explained everything about the parasite and the pill that the small pharmaceutical company designed. They were apparently a small business, and with this pill, they saved the entire world from the "flesh eater" pandemic, a moniker appropriately given to the parasite.

Catherine told me how hundreds of thousands of people had been affected and the parasite spread all over the world, reaching all the continents. But then this small company made a pill with the meager resources they had and saved the world. Not only did they save the world from the flesh eater, but they also created something capable of curing almost any kind of ailment. Their success launched them into fame overnight and investors flocked to have their research done by the company.

We needed more companies like those in the world – ones that selflessly focused on saving the mankind, and not just earning cash.

Anyway, coming back to the sardonic sense of humor. I had become obsessed with rubbing my skin until it was bloody whenever I felt like there might be a bug crawling there. Just the memory of having those things crawling inside my eyeballs, ears, and mouth made me feel sick.

But then I started to joke about it in front of the doctors. They already looked at me like I was this maggot-infested and highly contagious animal, so I might as well try and cheer myself up.

It worked, but only after a while.

Hey, doc? Got any rice on the menu? That way it'll be hard for me to differentiate whether I'm eating maggots or real food.

Stand back, I gotta sneeze. Don't want maggots and snot all over you, do you?

"We ran your blood tests, stool samples, and urine samples, and you're clean," Regina said.

"I'm clean?" I asked, wanting to make sure I heard it right.

"Yes, Melanie." Regina's smile grew wider. "You're almost free to go."

I hopped to my feet and hugged Regina. She was taken aback but didn't resist. She patted me on the back and let out a chuckle. After she gave me all the details about when I can leave and what I should do to stay safe, I thanked her for everything.

"You'll be immune for the next six months or so, but if you notice anything unnatural, any open wounds or something that you think shouldn't be there, go to your nearest hospital immediately and they'll run tests."

"Thank you so much."

Needless to say, the day dragged on, as it always did whenever the finish line was in sight. The doctors ran a few more tests on me that day, and in the morning, I was dismissed. Catherine was waiting for me at the gate.

It felt good being out in the fresh air again. I was a little apprehensive about every bug and bird I've seen flying above me, but Catherine was there to assure me everything would be all right. We sat in the car and she drove me home.

"Hey, what happened to Darren? I haven't heard from him since… before the flesh-eating pandemic started," I said.

"I'm sorry, Melanie," Catherine said. "He died from the parasite."

Shit.

I couldn't help but feel like I was partly responsible for his death. His death hurt me more than I was willing to admit. I had liked him a lot and had really thought we were going to have something special. I hoped he was in a better place now.

Nothing special happened after that.

I went back to work – we worked from home because of the parasite – I started living a healthier lifestyle, and I was going out on a date in a few days with a guy I met in a Zoom meeting. The world was stabilizing and the cases of the parasite were decreasing thanks to the magic pill. Everything was going great. There was only one thing that still bothered me.

Sometimes, I woke up at night to feel pain in my wrist. Pain, and something deep under my skin.

Something that feels like squirming.

LAB PART 7

"Thank you for coming down here on such short notice, Mr. Myers," Doctor Simmons said with a courteous bow of the head.

Andrew Myers cleared his throat. He hated conducting these visits to the company. Everybody treated him with politeness, and somehow at the same time, revulsion. He felt both welcome and as an intruder.

He didn't complain. He understood why they hated having him there, as all the other establishments of the company did. It was his job to make sure everything was functioning properly and up to standard. Essentially, he was never here to tell an office what a great job they were doing. He was here to find faults in the way it operated.

"I'd like to get started immediately, if that's all right with you, Doctor Simmons," Andrew said, curt and expressionless.

He had learned early on that the polite approach in this line of work changed nothing.

"Of course. Right this way, Mr. Myers" Simmons said as he gestured to the door leading toward the quarantine.

Andrew held a notepad firmly in his hand, the pen tapping the paper, ready to take notes of anything he found inadequate. When they walked past the panes of glass that overlooked the laboratories, he stopped to scrutinize the area.

The scientists in the room were intently focused on a petri dish in front of them, discussing something with visible vigor.

Andrew knew it was just a ruse. The company offices scheduled for inspection were never as impeccable as what Andrew saw. He knew firsthand how hectic everything becomes at the office the moment inspection schedules an arrival.

Cleaners scrub the place until it's completely sterilized, the low-performing and nervous employees are given a day off while the good ones stay at work pretending to do something important that they'd undoubtedly rehearsed a dozen or so times, everyone is run through a scenario of what to do or say when Andrew arrives, and so on.

"What are they working on?" Andrew asked, pointing to the scientists on the other side of the glass.

"Running some tests on the PT-104. The higher-ups believe there's more potential in the parasite," Simmons recited.

The statement came out as too fluent, too smooth. *Rehearsed,* Andrew figured.

They went on toward the test subjects' wing. Doctor Simmons put on a face mask. Andrew, in his position, had the privilege of not having to wear protective equipment if he didn't want to. He never got into contaminated areas, anyway.

As they entered the subjects' wing, Andrew took a look at each test subject in the cell, taking notes of what Simmons was guiding him through.

A young boy with warts all over his body, a middle-aged woman with skin that looked stone-hardened, a patient whose gender or age Andrew couldn't discern due to the swollen skin that looked like the person had been stung by a million bees.

Then when they reached the cell number six, Andrew recognized the patient. The man was seated on his bed, catatonically looking in front of him. Physically, nothing seemed wrong with him save the blank stare.

"Is that Doctor Curtis?" Andrew asked.

"Oh, I suppose you weren't informed?" Simmons asked.

"About what?"

"Doctor Curtis' performance has been… less than satisfactory as of late."

"I see. What's wrong with him?"

"It's a new type of worm we're testing. I take it you're familiar with *toxoplasma gondii*?"

Andrew gave a brusque nod.

"We're still in the initial stages, but we believe that we've finally found a way to have a parasite control the human brain activities, similarly to how *t. gondii* controls rodents," Simmons said.

"Interesting," Andrew said and jotted down some notes. "Tell me more."

"As I said, we're still in the initial stages of the experiment. Thanks to the funds raked in by the PT-104, the company has been able to invest into this experiment. Doctor Curtis' mind right now is struggling for control against the worm. He's aware of everything, but he cannot control his motor functions. In about seven days or so, the worm will completely take over and Doctor Curtis will continue acting like a normal human being."

"Oh?" Andrew raised an eyebrow.

"We have high hopes for this experiment. Unlike the PT-104, the worm is able to take complete control of the host and continue living its life. Not only that, but it can mimic the host's speech, body language, habits, everything. Essentially, it can hijack the host's brain and continue living the host's life without ever alerting the host's loved ones."

"What happens to the host?"

"At some point, the host will die."

"But the worm will be able to continue controlling the host's body?"

"Exactly. It is the perfect parasite. Almost impossible to detect, extremely intelligent, and able to mimic the host to very subtle details."

Andrew cast an aloof glance at Doctor Curtis. The subject hadn't moved an inch since the moment Andrew arrived.

For a protracted moment, Andrew thought about the whole thing. A world full of zombie-like humans living everyday lives as normally as they would, working their nine to five jobs, paying taxes, taking kids to football practice… all the while being controlled by a worm.

"That is very impressive, Doctor Simmons. I can see why you were promoted. I will make sure to mention your hard work to my superiors," Andrew said.

"Thank you, Mr. Myers," Simmons said with a hint of surprise.

"When do you expect the worm to be launched into the test phase?"

"Two months, tops."

"I look forward to seeing the results."

"Let's proceed, shall we? I still have so many things to show you, Mr. Myers," Simmons said with a wide grin.

About Boris Bacic

Boris Bacic is a prolific author who has been writing stories for years, ranging from genres like horror, sci-fi, mystery, thriller, and suspense, several of them becoming bestsellers. He has been praised widely as an author who constructs compelling narratives and plots that will keep you at the edge of your seat. His stories regularly find their way among the top posts on Nosleep and he's had dozens of his stories narrated by famous Creepypasta Youtube narrators. His stories are guaranteed to make your blood run cold, give you a feeling of paranoia or make you sleep with your lights on, but will also get you attached to the characters, making you feel like you're right there with them in their predicament.

Other BDP books by Boris Bacic

Until Undeath Do Us Part
Terrifying Love - A Halloween Anthology
Beautiful Tragedy - A Halloween Anthology
The Witch of the Woods